Praise for J O S E P H   H U R K A ' S
Fields of Light: A Son Remembers His Heroic Father
and *Before: A Novel.*

FOR *Fields of Light: A Son Remembers His Heroic Father (2001, 2013):*
WINNER OF THE PUSHCART EDITORS' BOOK AWARD

"Gripping ... what emerges—in addition to Hurka's respect for his father—are the difficult choices that Communism forced onto individuals and the dignity that was still possible ... This fine memoir is the winner of Pushcart's 19th Annual Editors' Book Award." *–PUBLISHERS WEEKLY STARRED REVIEW*

"A riveting read." *–THE CHICAGO TRIBUNE*

"Hurka ... writes of the deep human instinct to survive ... *Fields of Light* is about courage." *–THE BLOOMSBURY REVIEW*

"It's the story of a man who fought for democracy and ... the moving account of a son who finally comes to know his father." *–BOOKLIST*

"Hurka's singular effort has helped reestablish the memoir as an important tool of discovery." *–THE BOSTON GLOBE*

"Joseph Hurka...offers a generous, kind, and thoughtful memoir about his desire to inhabit his father Josef's past, and thereby give both of them a form of new life. Laced with the history of the Czech Republic—a mosaic of oppression, resistance, rebellion and survival—*Fields of Light: A Son Remembers His Heroic Father* portrays the literal journey Hurka takes to the Czech Republic to trace his father's footsteps, and the figurative journey that is every traveler's voyage of discovery." *–PLOUGHSHARES*

"Joseph Hurka's *Fields of Light* is an exceptional memoir ... that rare entry ... dealing with the details of life under Communism and the resistance of simple patriots, who dared to follow the spirit of democracy ... " *–VERA LASKA, INTERNATIONAL JOURNAL ON WORLD PEACE*

"In a poignant style that gracefully interweaves thoughts from a travel diary on Hurka's pilgrimage to modern Prague with dream sequences and bitter historical reality, the author traces the terrible and glorious history of the Czech Republic through the lives of his family and particularly his father … the reader comes away with the feeling that in the quest for freedom there are very few ordinary people. Recommended for all collections." –*LIBRARY JOURNAL*

FOR *Before: A Novel (2007):*

"A beautifully-written novel that, rather astonishingly, manages to weave together memory, loss, youth, hope and evil into a compelling story that spans generations. There are echoes upon echoes in this haunting tale." –*ANITA SHREVE, author of* STELLA BAIN

"Like Chekhov or Carver, Hurka is able to make us feel empathy for these people by showing that these people are us … like all great art, *Before* challenges, and even disturbs, the way you think and feel about the world and yourself. Like all of life's important experiences, reading this book will not leave you unscathed but it will leave you closer to whole." –*MATT W. MILLER, author of* CLUB ICARUS, *WINNER OF THE VASSAR MILLER PRIZE IN POETRY*

"Set in the lengthening shadows of the twentieth century and the stark sunlight of the twenty-first, Joseph Hurka's *Before* brilliantly illuminates not only our capacity to do one another great and lasting harm but also our innate desire to rise above the darkness with courage and grace and an enduring faith in what is truly possible in ourselves." –*ANDRE DUBUS III, author of* DIRTY LOVE

"Hurka has accomplished what seems impossible—he has created three very different characters whose stories smoothly interact into an emotional, frightening and compelling novel … beautiful writing." –*DESERET MORNING NEWS*

"A powerful and fearless novel about the violent histories people carry into exile—and the way memory continues to haunt, even after decades of peace. Intense, often frightening, ultimately redemptive." –*PETER ORNER, author of* LOVE AND SHAME AND LOVE

"*Before* shows us two men shaped by war trauma, haunted by vivid memories, and driven to extremes—of kindness and evil. The writing carries a deep and swift energy." *NEENAH ELLIS, PUBLIC RADIO PRODUCER, author of* IF I LIVE TO BE 100: LESSONS FROM THE CENTENARIANS

"A stunning novel of intrigue and delight. You read this book as if watching a film: the visuals are spectacular, and the meaning of the story reverberates in your mind long after." –*F.D. REEVE, author of* MY SISTER LIFE

GRACEFUL LIES

twelve stories

by

JOSEPH HURKA

WILD CREEK PRESS
NEW HAMPSHIRE

WILD CREEK PRESS
wildcreekpress@hotmail.com

Author website:
www.josephhurka.com

PUBLISHER'S NOTE

Grateful acknowledgment is made to the publications in which these stories first appeared, some in slightly different form: "Doberman" in *Agni;* "After The Hurricane" in *The Larcom Review;* "Robert Robert Robert" in *Tufts Magazine* and *Entelechy International;* "The Great White Bluesman" in *Alaska Quarterly Review;* "The Angry Boy" in *Out of the Blue Writers Unite,* and in an anthology edited by Andre Dubus, called *Into The Silence;* "Her Lover" and "Luna" in *Entelechy International;* "The Candidate" in *The Dos Passos Review;* "Yank" in *Ploughshares,* and "Light Wings" in *Roger.*

"Wolf's head" image © Advent, 2013, and used under license from Shutterstock.com. "Field of grass through sunset" (cover art) © Nature Art, and used under license from Shutterstock.com. Author photograph (back cover) by Diane Lord. Lyrics to "Bandit of Love" and "Say You're Mine" © 2015 Joseph Hurka. The excerpt on page 73 is from "God Appears at Night as a Burning Field," from Seven-Star Bird, *© 2003 David Daniel, published by Graywolf Press, Saint Paul, Minnesota. The quote on page 47 is from Jules Verne's* 20,000 Leagues Under the Sea, *originally published in 1871.*

FOR ANDRE DUBUS
KEEP FISHING, SANTIAGO.

CONTENTS

I am circling around God, around the ancient tower,
and I have been circling for a thousand years,
and I still don't know if I am a falcon, or a storm,
or a great song.

RAINER MARIA RILKE
The Book Of Hours: Love Poems To God

DOBERMAN

IN the late summer evening, the two boys and the father came to a meadow. One boy had his father's eyes and walk; the other boy was a friend.

They had been going around the pond nearby and now they were heading home. They came to a knoll. The sun was shining brown-gold on the dry weeds and grass. Jediah Vest felt his father's hand around his own, and when he glanced behind he could see, through trees, the silver water in the sun. It looked very bright and he could not watch it for long.

He could smell the dry ground. The sun was not as hot on his back as it had been when they were at the pond.

Billy was telling Jediah's father a story, something about baseball, and how Billy had stolen second. Jediah's father said Wow, Billy, you're getting fast. That's the way to do it.

Crabapple trees hissed in the meadow, and past those branches was the dark forest with the path to Jediah's neighborhood. The pine trees were like towers with patches of bright sky behind them. The sky was the color of orange flowers Jediah's mother grew in her garden. Jediah thought of his mother in the kitchen, looking out the window at the forest, making dinner.

Careful on the embankment, Jediah's father said. Jediah felt his father's hand tighten. The boys swung out on the father's arms, swaying over the steepness for a moment; the grass stirred below them, and Jediah's insides leapt. His father laughed with them, carrying them down the few feet, and landed them at the bottom. Here grass grew every which way as high as Jediah's waist, looking as if it were on fire. You could smell the apples and the dry ground. Dragonflies went up and down and sideways.

Okay boys, Jediah's father said. That's enough swinging on the old man. You're getting too big for me now.

The crabapple trees were black and twisted when you got near them. Crabapples hung in green clusters above Jediah. He could hardly see anything in the bottom of the forest ahead because it was so dark there.

And then, while Jediah watched, the dark bottoms of the trees began to move. He felt his father's hand tighten again on his own.

Mrs. Woodrow's dogs got out, Jediah's father said, quietly. Okay, boys.

The dogs came from the forest, eight of them. They paused and stared. They sniffed the ground and came on again, their black heads and small ears nodding with the running. Jediah could not swallow.

Jediah had seen the dogs up close in old Mrs. Woodrow's cage once, behind wire mesh. One, larger than the others, had showed its teeth and snarled and barked and the others barked and the barking went right into your stomach and Jediah had stepped back to his father's legs and Mrs. Woodrow clucked her tongue and laughed and told the dogs how silly they were. Jediah's father had led Jediah away from the cage quickly. They had gone inside Mrs. Woodrow's very old home. Everything had smelled like candles there. Jediah had felt his father being polite to Mrs. Woodrow, as they sat with tea. The tea was too hot to hold or drink for a while. The window looked out at the large, ivy-covered cage with the dogs.

Now Jediah's father firmly lifted Billy, then Jediah, into the nearest crabapple tree. Jediah felt the swift pull under his shoulders, and when he was in the first branches he grabbed hold of the harsh wood and felt his father's hands leave him. Billy said, Mr. Vest?

It's all right, Billy, Jediah's father said. Both of you boys climb up a little higher. You're good at that.

The dogs came up to the tree and surrounded it and Jediah's father. The big one put its paws up on the trunk and barked suddenly and so loudly that Jediah felt it in his stomach, something coming up in his throat. The dog snarled and showed its white teeth. Billy said, Mr. Vest?

It's all right, Billy, Jediah's father said again. Keep climbing. You're fine there. He said, Stay there, boys. Don't come down until I'm back. I shouldn't be long. Dogs, *come*.

The dog on the tree looked back, hesitated, and then dropped to the ground. It went up to Jediah's father to sniff, but Jediah's father was already walking for the pines. The other dogs sniffed the ground, glanced up at the boys, and turned toward the path. Jediah watched his father walk with the dogs around him into the forest. He heard his father talking to them as if they were guests at a party. Then the trees were over them and he could not see his father anymore.

A few nights before, when Jediah's father got home from his job at the yacht yard, there was an awful fight in the kitchen. It was something about a party and Jediah's father was going to be God-damned if he would go be with those people. Jediah's mother's voice rose and she was crying. Jediah went down the stairs carefully and he heard his father say I'm in no mood and his mother said Well maybe Henry for once you're going to *hear this,* her voice hoarse and sad like if she had a cold. Jediah waited at the banister and he could see the kitchen doorway and he could not breathe well. He saw a dish fly by, heard it smash, and it was suddenly like the whole house was coming apart. The smooth paint of the spindle posts grew wet from Jediah's face and hands. His parents heard him and came and brought him up to their bed and he lay face down on a pillow while his mother rubbed his back. His father paced awkwardly and said, I'm sorry, son, parents are stupid sometimes, but don't worry, we're not going to go do some stupid damned thing. Jediah had thought about how Billy's father lived now in a house by the sea. Billy had said there was a big window there where you could watch the motorboats. Sometimes

Billy's father drove him all that way to school, and from the high windows of the bus Jediah saw his friend get dropped off.

Don't worry, son, Jediah's father said, his hand in Jediah's hair. *That's right,* his mother said. She made circles on his back. *That's right, little man. No more fighting.* Soon Jediah could breathe steadily again and the windows were dark. When he woke, still in their bed, he could hear his parents' voices low in the kitchen. He could hear a car pass on the street. The car lights moved in squares over the wall.

Billy made a sound in his throat. We're high up, he said, looking at the ground. The fire in the grass was going out. The pond was darker, and Jediah could not see the colors as much now through the trees. He felt wind against his cheek and wood biting into his forearms where he held onto his branch. He could smell the apples and the water. The birds seemed suddenly to be talking a lot, saying things and answering one another. The wind rushed once hard and the tree groaned and rocked and the ground seemed to rise.

We're moving, Billy said.

We're all right, Jediah said. He looked down at the meadow. Think about hitting baseballs, Billy.

Billy closed his eyes, but Jediah didn't really know if his friend was thinking about swinging a bat. He thought of his father in the dark forest with the dogs. He wished his father had a bat.

The insects grew louder, the whole field of them. The flattened places of grass where his father and the dogs had gone were very hard to see.

Maybe we can get down now, Billy said.

No, Jediah said. He said for us to stay here.

Billy closed his eyes and gripped his branch, for the wind was gusting. Jediah watched the face of his friend. Then he watched the forest carefully until he could see his father's shoulders, a steady movement, coming from the dark trees of summer.

AFTER THE HURRICANE

AFTER the hurricane, in the morning when it was still, Frank Robb woke from a dream because he knew, suddenly, that his wife had not slept. Diana lay beside him, a light summer blanket covering half of her body, and she was running her fingers absently over her breasts and staring at the ceiling. Frank Robb had been dreaming that he was swimming high in the air over the rural Massachusetts town where they lived, and he still saw the violence of the storm as if it were below him: trees split and splintered, telephone poles tilted and cracked, telephone lines down and leaves swept across roads.

His wife stared at the ceiling. He leaned over to kiss her neck. He felt her heartbeat in the pulse of the artery there. He laced his fingers into the fingers of one of her hands and kissed the corner of one eye. Still she looked upward.

"Maybe you could do it with a surrogate," she said, "like in one of those sci-fi movies or these weird legal cases."

"Stop it," he told her, into her ear. "Just stop it there."

She rolled away from him and he rubbed her back and neck with his hands. He kissed the back of her head, where wispy hair met skin. He saw the creases below her jawline, and other creases running toward her eye in that pale morning light. After a while he felt her move into sleep.

When she was breathing steadily, he rose from the bed. He put on his silk bathrobe, for it was cool this September morning, after the hurricane. He put another blanket over his wife. He looked out the window and it resembled his dream: the stone driveway through the woods scattered with leaves and twigs and branches. There was an oak tree down across the drive, blocking their way to the road beyond, and the old garage was still nailed shut with boards against the blow.

They had secured the garage just as the storm had come in last night. He smiled, thinking of it: Diana watching the local news station and saying, Come here, honey. The news people saying the storm would solidly hit the area, sixteen miles in from the sea. Diana saying, The garage will blow open for sure. And so they'd made a wild, evening run through hard rain, purple glimpses of sky behind trees, the rain soaking Frank Robb's neck as they ran for the building, tore open doors; he had searched for strapping and nails and hammer, handed the strapping to Diana, and then they were out of the darkness of the garage and into the rain again and Diana laughed as she fumbled with the long pieces of wood and Frank Robb nailed, barely able to see the hammer striking nails, and he'd laughed uncontrollably too and clutched his soaked wife in the storm, watching her closed eyes, her bright teeth, her blind face smiling up at him and at the rain.

Four hours later they had listened to the radio in bed, the electricity out and the strange howl of the hurricane around them. Frank Robb held his wife closer when the announcer spoke of the houses to the north, on the ocean, that had blown into the sea. When lightning flashed he caught their reflections in the flooded window: white, surprised figures staring out at the fury, clutching one another. They'd laughed at this too, and then made love as they had not for a long time, Diana's hands tight on Frank Robb's back as the rain drummed and whipped against the siding of the house.

He put on jeans now and a pair of worn leather loafers and a t-shirt and wind jacket and went downstairs and out into the bright, dry day. The cicadas whistled and buzzed through the clean air. He went to the garage and found the hammer where he'd left it, by the cement foundation at the side of the building. Then, with the nails shrieking through the relative quiet of the forest, he wedged the strapping from the wooden doors.

Inside, their two cars sat pristine, metal dark like cool glass; the Robbs kept their foreign automobiles washed all the time, sleek and pretty in that dim garage. Each weekday these machines brought them to work, whistling through dry leaves and toward the skyline of Boston, then into the city, bringing Diana to the downtown advertising firm and Frank Robb to the small college in the Back Bay where he taught. He loved his autumn drives, the escape of them, the rush through color in the country, and the lucky flow of city traffic if you got in at an odd hour—dipping under the old bridges as if you were part of a river of metal, with the sun somber on the Charles River beside you, reminding you that winter was not long in coming.

He went behind the cars now and found his axe. He walked out into the green brightness and started chopping at the fallen oak, the sweat coming to his neck and chest and lower back, the wood chips flying in the sunshine. The tree was about a half a foot thick, and he needed the steadiness of this activity, the way it made his chest hurt and his biceps ache. He looked back at the house, thinking he might see Diana up in the window watching him, but she was not there.

He glanced at the town road. The road crews had segmented a large tree that had fallen close to their driveway entrance; he remembered hearing their distant work in the night as he'd dreamed. The big tree lay in pieces at the side of the street, thick and white at the cuts. He thought about getting one of those chain saws: he'd always fancied them when he'd seen them in department stores, their rugged teeth somehow promising a newer, more rigorous life. He imagined the feel of such a machine in his hands, the powerful vibration and sound. He resumed working, and sometimes his axe mis-struck with a dull sound against the wood. But most of the time it bit cleanly, cleaving the white V below him. He kept his eyes on the oak as the axe cut more deeply into its rings, and wondered: what was happening *this* year, had he left the public relations firm to go teach? And *this* one, this darker circle, had they met for the first time in college?

9

Each strike of the axe took him more deeply into his forty-one years.

Even with the tree halved, he could barely slide both sections of it off to the sides of the driveway. He grunted and hefted until they were enough out of the way to let the cars get through. He would call the small yard-work business in town later and get them to saw up the two lengths for winter firewood. He wiped his arm across his forehead, and looked up again at his blond, modern home. The previous structure on the property, a hideous old bungalow, had been torn down immediately when they'd bought the place seven years ago: Frank Robb remembered that its dark green color had blended like mud with the forest and that some of the porch boards had fallen to powder. The house he and Diana had constructed in its place offered a stark, clean contrast to their many surrounding trees, and to the patches of blue sky beyond where the foliage had been thinned by the storm. The leaves that remained in the forest had kicked over into brilliant color: burnished scarlets and oranges that glowed as if from some inner light.

He looked in on Diana and she had drawn the shades and gone back to sleep and now, after the bright outdoors, he could just barely make out her form. He went near the bed and put his hands on his knees and listened intently until he could hear the rhythmic rise and fall of her breathing.

***

Five weeks before, after an ectopic pregnancy that had nearly taken Diana Robb's life, the Robbs' doctor had met with them in Diana's hospital room. *There are many children out there who need good homes,* he'd said, *and you should begin considering that, or surrogacy.* The doctor had shaken his head sadly, his hand firm and small on the railing of Diana's hospital bed, when Diana told him she still wanted to try for a traditional pregnancy. *The time is passing, Diana, and it's just becoming too dangerous,* he'd said. Diana kept her composure there, but two evenings later, at home, she suddenly slammed the refrigerator door in the kitchen and cried and said, *I'm not a woman.* Frank Robb had spoken softly to his wife: he took her elbow gently and moved her to the living room couch. He drew her close and felt the wetness of her eyes against his throat. Outside the windows, in the gloaming, the trees still held the dark, deep green of summer, but he'd hardly seen them. Instead, with her weight and grief in the circle of his arms, he remembered the many nights of creams and spermicide during those years when they had not wanted children: when Diana had told him that her life would not be defined by children. Frank Robb had agreed: he hadn't felt ready to be a father. He'd used cool, lubricated condoms that made him fight to maintain erections; Diana had slipped those rubbers off expertly between her fingers after their lovemaking, and tested them by filling them with water in the bathroom sink. She had shown him this once, as he'd watched her from the bed; she'd leaned against the doorjamb of the bathroom and held up an engorged, drooping condom in-between her fingertips for him to see. The bathroom light had been on behind her and Frank Robb had seen the milky fluid swimming within the water, glowing and translucent. They'd laughed about it, he remembered.

Watching the darkening summer forest with his grieving wife these few weeks ago, Frank Robb was moved to stunning tears by the memory of that laughter, for it seemed to confirm the presence of some conspiracy against them, to echo the joy of some enemy. Diana had shifted away from him and stared at him, at his tears, with baffling, accusatory anger, as if discovering a betrayal of his. She searched his face, hard, and for a moment he panicked, thinking he might, somehow, have actually wronged her.

"What *is* it, darling?" he'd said.

But she'd gone on staring, and her stare had softened, and she'd wiped the mascara from her cheeks with her hands, closed her eyes, and touched her husband's face with her fingers.

Long after the trees were black that night, Frank Robb had held his wife.

***

On this Sunday morning after the hurricane he made bacon and eggs, thinking these smells might bring Diana down from the darkened room. But they did not and he reached into the refrigerator for orange juice, a cool rush of air as he closed the padded door. The front of the door was littered with newspaper clippings on stocks and finance, all anchored by motivational and philosophical magnets. *A woman without a man is like a fish without a bicycle,* read one. *Serious Diet in Progress,* read another; *Enter At Your Own Risk.* Their kitchen was large and spacious: they'd drawn it carefully for the architect, their pencil lines creating the space that they would one day live in, love in, dine in. Frank Robb set a placemat at the kitchen counter and sat on one of the stools and read the previous day's *Globe* and had his breakfast.

The clock on the microwave was a blinking set of zeroes, a steady, blue-crystal pulse. He decided he would fix it later. He read about the impending hurricane and a Mideast peace conference. He riffled through to sports, where the Red Sox were making a last gasp at glory. In the *North Shore* section there was a feature about a ninety-five year-old lobster found off the coast of Beverly a few days before. The man who discovered the creature had returned it to the ocean, saying that it ought to live out its days there, instead of like some freak in an aquarium. The lobster, the newspaper said, still bore young.

Frank Robb put the paper down and looked up at the clock. Its insistence disturbed him, and he found he could not bear watching it. He looked out the kitchen windows. The trees were stirring briskly, there, in the bright day. He thought of his wife upstairs, the shades drawn, of how nothing he could say could bring her out of her sadness these past weeks; only last night had been different, a charge of recklessness they hadn't felt in years. He felt—he couldn't help it—strengthened, refreshed this morning, despite the sadness in the house. He was a little ashamed of his levity.

Later, he thought, *I'll change into sweats and sneakers. I'll take the car.* He imagined himself threading his way out through fallen trees and branches. In the world beyond their driveway he would drive the car smoothly and maybe he would have to stop sometimes and pull debris from the streets. He would do this happily, in the smells of clean car and wet forest, of tar and sunshine. Then he could be on the highway, and twenty minutes later at the sea. He could run on its sands, alone and alive, and the swollen waves beside him would be that pearl color that they always were after storms. He could run and run.

He put his plate and cup in the sink and stepped upstairs, quietly, stopping just before the bedroom door. He stayed there a moment, staring at its solid, wood-grained surface. He touched the door with the tips of his fingers.

He turned and went down the hall, to the office they had planned to convert into a child's room. It was a small room with only a desk and a laptop and a chair facing a wall-length window. Glancing out at the clear, shadowed space that was their yard, he thought about the raking he would actually be doing later, and he was grateful for their old decision not to let grass grow beneath their many trees. They had a yard of crushed bark, and he had never regretted it, watching neighbors sit and sweat on mowers.

Here, on the desk, was the row of bills he had laid out the day before. He sat and turned on the computer and opened his checkbook and paid department stores and banks where they had credit card accounts. He paid for their cars and a new septic tank; he paid clothing stores. He absorbed himself in the sureness of this work, this giving a fresh order to things. He threw away advertisements and enticements to buy more.

He came to the latest medical bill. He broke it open and looked at the even, impersonal typing across the page, the exactness of his wife's name next to a printed column titled, *Services Performed*. He lay it before him.

Frank Robb stared at the page, his fists clenched on either side of him. The bill seemed to grow large, the numbers there, the abbreviated descriptions of procedures. He saw Diana saying to the doctor that she still wanted to try for a traditional pregnancy; he had a strange sense of rising, of moving out and above himself to the height of those few remaining leaves, a flight like that of his dream. *Time is passing.* The doctor had said the phrase in the time it took a heart to begin beating. That knowledge, of passing time, had always been with Frank Robb, a dark bird sailing. He had ignored this truth he'd known. Standing by his wife's hospital bed that day, his hand lightly holding her shoulder in support, he'd thought about how, secretly, he'd always been grateful for the lack of complication Diana's choices had given him. And then shame had come, this same shame he lived with now, beneath everything he did. The same as when, at parties, people had asked about children, and Diana had said, *Soon. We've been making plans.* Frank Robb had sipped bourbon at those gatherings, after those questions, and thought of his freedom and avoided eyes and watched the ice in his glass; he'd felt the heat of his face and his wife's pride, year after year, beside him.

Truth had been there, the dark bird circling for another pass, and later in those evenings after he'd made love it was always there. And when he'd rolled over gratefully to peace and sleep it hovered at the edge of his consciousness, a feather-breath of wings among leaves brightening before death.

It was here now, in this house, in the form of his sleeping wife down the hall.

Frank Robb found he could not swallow, and he was having trouble catching his breath. He got up quickly and walked down the hallway and opened the door to the bedroom. The shades were still drawn, but with his eyes adjusted to the dimmer light of the house he could see Diana clearly now, the sheets and blankets tangled about her figure. He went to the bed and knelt on the floor before her. She was in a heavy sleep and he moved forward and touched her forehead with his own. He closed his eyes and stayed with her for a long time like that, as if joined with her in some silent, mutual prayer.

THE HUNT

I HAVE a photograph of her, so many years ago, this professor who had an affair with me. I was twenty, on fire; she was thirty-two, teaching English, wife of a world-renowned architect. In this particular shot (it was my composition, for I was in photography class as well) you see the professor's face in profile, a near-silhouette against a dark, intricate stone wall. My intent was to capture the contrast of her smoothness and beauty against that background; even so, even knowing what I was up to, it is alarming to see how striking a woman she is—full lips, balanced nose, a great, wide eye.

In our classroom in that private Massachusetts college she was buttoned-down, demure. There was a powerful sensuality to her, an inescapable grace to her violet eyes, to her tapered forearms and precise fingers. Her lips sometimes parted slightly when she listened to your responses. College boys grew quiet around her; college girls checked her over carefully: you caught them sizing up the professor's bright engagement ring, her simple wedding band.

The classroom was seventies-modern: full glass walls braced by cement columns. There was a small pond with a bridge outside, silver and black water shining. The professor broke its light with her profile, her cascade of dark-blond hair. She paced across the windows, speaking of Gatsby's hunger, and I could imagine the Great Man on a night of revelry, tossing his beautiful shirts before Daisy. There was a simple truth represented here, my professor said: *that a man falls for the dance of nature, and lays his gifts before a woman. A woman accepts or rejects, and the species goes on or does not.*

Strangely, though there were some hard-core feminists in the class, I don't remember any objections to my professor's philosophy. Was it because she, herself, was such a force of nature?

We followed the arc of Gatsby's passion until he drifted through his pool, trailing blood: until the billboard eyes of Doctor T.J. Eckleburg stared over the American tragedy, the forgotten valley of ashes.

Outside our seminar windows fall was coming, the trees each day a more burnished red. I watched the professor's lips, her body, move against that autumn light. I came up and asked questions after class. I felt her evaluate the uniformity of my high cheekbones, the cleft of my chin.

At the Haverhill Ale Room—an Irish eatery by day, a pub and stage for local rock bands by night—the professor and I sat in a booth one afternoon, three weeks into the semester. She had suggested we continue a literary conversation we'd started after class. I watched her glance around now, preparing to say something secretive. Waitresses stepped by us, keeping up with orders; businessmen nearby played darts. There was a jukebox spinning out hits. Outside the windows the Merrimack River flowed by, slow and dark.

The professor spoke of her husband. I had to look at her lips carefully to catch everything; he was a visionary, she said, and constantly in demand for speeches and presentations. This week he was at a conference in Los Angeles.

"He's a genius, no question. He's amazing at what he does," she said. "I've always admired him. But we're best friends now, nothing more—"

"Why so?" I said.

"He prefers men to women," she said. "I didn't find out until two years into the marriage."

"You must have been angry."

"Yes," she said, "at first. But I also saw that he'd struggled with it all his life. His father and brother were the same. It was like some darkness in their family, something they all contended with."

Often now, the architect traveled to San Juan or San Francisco to meet with male lovers. My professor didn't share a bed with him anymore, she said—they had not been intimate for seven years. She'd thought, many times, of leaving. But she had her own section of the upper floor, and they got along well, and the arrangement seemed to work for both of them.

"I'm telling you things even my closest friends don't know," the professor said, watching my eyes closely, smiling a bit. Her teeth were very white. She ran a finger over the edge of her glass. "People think I live a charmed life. It isn't charmed. We just keep up a good front. But it works."

I felt her confession as a new geography we were entering. Lightness danced in my chest and throat.

We drove to the ocean that afternoon, my old Ford following her Porsche through stark dunes. We walked together in the cold of the shore wind. We kissed finally in a seaport bar. There was a mahogany-toned intimacy to the place: loud, blue-collar voices all around. The indifference of the surroundings seemed to endorse our illicit connection. My professor sat close to me, slipped a hand beneath my coat, kissed my neck. Her scent was of sandalwood.

The house she shared with the architect was twenty minutes from the sea; a sprawling, minimalist, blond-wood creation located on a ridge high above a ravine. A whitewater river ran through that cut in the earth. The house was decorated with the sleek Scandinavian furniture of the day. The professor's bedroom window ran floor to ceiling, looking over the twisting water, giving you this sense that you were flying dangerously, soaring.

She pulled me toward her bed, looked at my eyes with certainty. I had been with three college girls before; I had been told I was attractive enough, but my heart was in my ears. My professor didn't hesitate for my nervousness. She undid the

17

buttons of my shirt, pulled it away from me. Outside the light fell quickly; the ravine was soon dark and all you could see with any clarity was the tense white of the rapids below.

The next morning I got a few things from my apartment—a ramshackle set of rooms near the college that I shared with three other guys. I stayed with the professor much of that week, following her to and from campus, the Porsche growling ahead of me. In class, I watched her interact with students, the way my peers seemed to come alive as she gave them attention. I could still feel the naked twist and turn of her in bed—a motion my body kept reliving—but I made a good show of normalcy, volunteering my observations about Fitzgerald's *Babylon Revisited:* I surprised myself with what a good actor I could be.

Once, as I studied during evening hours in a library cubicle, I felt the professor come up behind me.

"Working hard?" she whispered.

"Very hard," I said.

Her lips were close to my neck, then my ear. "Time to come home and fuck me," she said.

I packed my things fast, nearly in a panic.

We made love and ate and talked and slept and woke and made love again. I lost track of hours, thinking of time as only dark and light, recognizing morning by the realization that birds were speaking in their mysterious languages, that the room was lightening—a background to my professor's emerging flesh, to our conversations. Late afternoon came as a great shadow over the ravine below. You didn't realize it was there until, suddenly, you sensed the darkening.

The professor wore oversized shirts and nothing else around me in her home. She made spaghetti with pesto and looked at me with mirth and didn't let her eyes leave mine as she dangled pasta over her mouth and took it with her tongue.

After the sex I would fall into a heavy sleep. Sometimes I woke in a fright, thinking I was hearing the crackling of stones, the architect's car in the driveway. Whatever their arrangement, I didn't want the man to walk in on us. But it was only wind against the clapboards of the house, leaves scurrying over that empty valley. My professor put a sleepy hand on me, lay a smooth palm on the back of my neck.

One night in that first week we rose and went through the home with a kind of archeological zeal. It was two a.m., a feeling like you were in some strange place between dream and reality. On the master bedroom dresser there was a framed headshot of the professor. She stared out with those haunting violet eyes, the sensual, coral-colored lips; she wore pearls. I avoided looking at another photo nearby, of husband and wife posed together.

Bracelets and necklaces were arranged in the thin dresser drawers below. My professor drew out a gold necklace, let it spill over her fingers like liquid. I had the uneasy sense, looking at all of it—the jewelry, the photographs, the teak and dark-blond and violet furnishings and bedspread—even the honey color of the walls—that the room and perhaps the whole house was a kind of shrine: that the architect lived in some unappeasable state of worship.

The elaborate walk-in closet was a large, hushed space filled with the architect's elegant suits, his overcoats shimmering behind plastic; on the opposing side were the professor's gowns from Oleg Cassini, Versace, Chanel. The professor touched these skins, told me they were just part of the staging, worn for nights of important gatherings. But she held one dress up to her body, revolved a bit in the floor-to-ceiling mirror. She looked like some film star from the nineteen-forties, I told her; she laughed, her eyes staying on herself. The lighting in the ceiling produced shadows over our features and when her eyes finally switched to mine she said that, in my black jeans, my unbuttoned shirt, I was like some beast emerging from the primal forest to claim her. I hunched my shoulders and acted it out, making her laugh again.

While my professor slept, later, I stared into the night. I imagined her—a frighteningly beautiful hostess, sitting on the carpeted living room steps downstairs that led to the deck. It was the end of a party; her wine was beside her, guests were gathered around her, everything more casual as the night drew to a close; everyone thinking how approachable she was, what an attractive pair she and the architect were. The small river was a furious white. The guests said goodnight, slowly filtered out. My professor nodded to her husband when it was done; the two of them shared a few words in the kitchen over wine, exchanging notes on the various personalities that had moved through their home. I envisioned my professor going up to the master bedroom and undressing and returning her pearls or gold to drawers, her dress to the closet. She took her pinot and, in her underwear, went down the hallway to her own quarters.

What did the architect see when he watched her near-nakedness? I imagined he waited at the bottom of the stairs for her to go by above. He was a mystery to me, with his shrine and his fine clothes and male lovers. Did he see her simply as a work of art, a possession?

II

Over time, when I thought about my professor in those dresses, when I imagined her at her husband's side in them, I grew angry. I understood that she wouldn't wear those skins for me.

My jealousy gave a savage edge to our intimacy. At an inn not far from the college I grabbed the professor's hair in my fist. I jerked her limbs around to adjust her on the bed in whatever position I wanted. A harsh, unfamiliar set of sounds came from my throat. The professor responded in kind, slapping me hard, this sudden flint in her eyes. She growled and bit me and we rolled and took turns holding each other down. We went into a dark place together, and when we turned over afterward, amazed, our hearts hammered like train wheels on a railroad.

I did not speak aloud of my jealousy, and I was sure the professor thought we had simply discovered a heightened passion. I suspect she was even proud of it—of bringing out this frenzy in her young lover. She kissed me frequently, leaned against me, and I liked to hear her laugh. We took walks on the winter ocean. We read books in the same spaces, either at the inn or at her house, and the professor was charmed by how absorbed I got in my reading, by my inability to find matching socks, my consistently uncombed hair. When she saw me walking down winter paths at the college she told me how jaunty I looked, how I seemed strong and ready for the world.

Sometimes after classes, when the architect was traveling, we lay on her bed at the house. Her books, encased in stately oak cabinets, stared at us from one wall. With the light on, the window was a dark reflection of us and I could not see the ravine. The professor pressed her body up behind me, her hands holding texts open before my eyes, her fingers caressing lines I needed to pay attention to. *No easy grades for you because you're fucking the professor,* she said. She tickled me and I would fight her off, hold her hands tightly. She spoke down into my ear, and in the window I could see the cascade of her hair over me. I would slowly let her hands free and she would push aside the book, unbutton and unzip my jeans, and she kept talking down into me that way, making me crazy.

I signed up for another semester with her, this time for a course titled *Literature After War,* an evening class. I decided on a major in what the college called Liberal Studies. Waiting in the registration line in old, elaborate Academy Hall, I overheard some guys behind me talking about what a *fucking fox* the professor was, how it was worth taking her class just to watch her. I sensed the strength of my secret—the knowledge I had of the professor's nakedness and passion. I possessed something, I was sure, that her husband did not; I felt like a powerful animal-king.

January came with snow, and we went to movies in nearby Lawrence, a depressed industrial area where there was little chance of our being discovered. We made out and groped each other in the back row like teenagers. The films flickered against the side of my professor's face, her hair, her neck and collarbone. Outside, homeless men wandered the parking lots with shopping carts full of their possessions. The row houses of the old mills were occupied by impoverished, broken families; gangs roamed the streets.

In the parking lot after the films, in the shadow of the Cineplex, we made love in the back seat of the Porsche, the professor's hair wild, framing her face above me, the windows misting over. She pounded my chest, bit me if I didn't keep up a steady enough rhythm for her as she closed in on her orgasm. She said, into my ear, *Keep going keep going don't you come yet you fuck.*

Once, the two of us still breathing hard, her face buried in my throat, we heard gunshots in the distance. I felt my professor's face rise. We were sweating, and she was turning to the sound, her nostrils flaring. We looked out the steamed windows as police lights, glittering blue, raced by through the drifting snow.

A few hours later we lay naked at the house, in the darkness.

"My father was a class-A prick," the professor was telling me. "A real son of a bitch. We were poor as shit. The Bible was his answer to everything."

We had showered after the Cineplex and she smelled of soap and the sandalwood. Beyond her silhouette the huge bedroom window stared at the river. The moon was out. Some large bird, a raptor, sailed briefly across the white and black: I could see its shadow move over the snowy sill. As she spoke the professor was a girl in Nebraska, in a house at the end of a dead-end road where she lived with her father. Her mother had died when she was an infant.

"He wanted me to be a boy," she said. "He was endlessly angry I wasn't."

For punishments, her father simply locked her in a pantry. He'd done this as long as she could remember. Sometimes he left her there for hours, in a darkness where she could not see. I saw her eyes glitter now with the terror of the memory.

She hated hunting, she said—seeing fresh death in the eyes of deer—but her father made her go. She remembered walking behind him with a Winchester rifle in her hands.

"I could have just put a bullet in his fucking head," she said. "Everybody would have believed it was an accident. I could have just killed the son of a bitch."

III

The guys in the apartment asked where I went when I disappeared for days at a time. I told them I was seeing an older woman. They whistled their approval. *Holy shit* and *Fuckin' A* and *How much older?* they said. *Thirty-two,* I said. I was duty-bound to keep it a secret, I told them, and they nodded and understood. But they said, *Goddamn, man,* and hit my biceps and there was respect and happiness in their eyes.

I felt like I was in some cold desert alone, not being able to tell them more. I sat at my bedroom window, looking over the mill town, the church yard below where I could see the back of Christ, His arms open. I said things to the professor in my mind; I rationalized things, made plans that couldn't come true. I thought of her constantly. Sometimes, when the architect was home and the professor had to entertain at his parties, I went for long walks in the cold, stomping off my frustration. I would imagine her in the beautiful dresses, the way she might touch her husband in moments of feigned intimacy. I stepped over the snowy sidewalks, jamming my hands in my coat pockets: pissed-off, fucked-up, missing her.

The photography helped. When the professor would let me, I took photographs of her, then spent hours in the red glow of the college darkroom, developing the images. I adjusted the Ilford paper in the developing solution with rubber tongs, switched it back and forth—and the professor emerged there, a strange, shimmering apparition. Her eyes always seemed to crystalize first, shining up at me from the solution.

Our new literature class discussed *All Quiet on the Western Front* and watched the 1930 film; we saw slides of Picasso's *Guernica* and read Hemingway's *The Sun Also Rises* and *A Farewell To Arms*. We wrote papers about unconditional love and what or whom you might give your life for. In the seminar room our reflections played out on the dark glass. Outside, in the winter cold, lights from the bridge were steady on the ice.

There was a night during this time: of snow coming down outside those windows, just as the seminar was ending; the professor handling the many student requests and last conversations that came her way. I left cheerily, handy with the mask I'd created; I waved to a couple of friends, put on my coat and scarf, chatting with some of the other students, then went down stairs and out to the parking lot. The snow squeaked beneath my feet, sparkling all around me. I started the engine of the Ford and waited behind the wheel, the heat just barely coming on, my breath rising. I rubbed my hands together, breathed hot air onto them; I watched students leave the building, making plans for the Ale Room, their breaths filtering through the library lights. They seemed miles from me now, distanced from me by this greater passion I had experienced. They started their cars and drove slowly off into the snow.

Then my professor, dressed in her leather winter coat, came down the steps. Her feet left the snow-sparkling earth, her car door shut. She started up the Porsche: I watched her brake lights flicker and go black again, and I followed her, threading through traffic. Everything in the winter night had a hushed, temporary quality to it, and I felt a rush of self-reliance; a certain rugged faith.

The architect was at a week-long conference in Berlin. Their house, high on that ridge, solidified now under the drifting storm. Inside, the living room fans whirled above us and we did not turn on the lights. The professor ripped my belt apart, undid my button and zipper, plunged a hand onto me. She grasped me tightly, making me gasp. She watched my eyes, regarding me. When she did things like this, when she looked at me in this cool, detached way, something in me broke loose and wild.

I fell into a troubled sleep later. I dreamed I was in a darkness so complete that I could not see any form, no matter how much I struggled to widen my eyes. I tried to speak, but couldn't articulate anything; my speech came out as a low, disconnected moan. I woke with desperate tears on my cheekbones. The professor was not in bed with me. I wiped my face quickly and got up.

An unsteady amber light came from the living room below the stairs: candles. I went down and the professor was at a desk, in a light robe, reading a pile of letters. She had one foot up on her chair, and she touched her lips absently to a naked knee as she considered the pages. Her hair was in disarray, and she swept it from her face now, looking at me.

"You okay?" she said.

"Nightmare," I said.

"I heard," she said.

I sat on the leather Scandinavian couch and she handed me letters as she finished with them. We read them through in the candlelight. They were written in her husband's strong hand, postmarked over the last year from Berlin, San Juan, Miami. The most recent, from San Francisco two weeks before, described a new disease, a failure of the immune system that was sweeping the homosexual community.

People are dying, Leslie, the architect wrote, *Five men just last week in LA. It doesn't seem to change what goes on in the bathhouses. Men go at each other like heterosexual men would go at women, if there were no rules of civility. There is this yearning out there, everybody on the hunt.*

The letters mentioned actors I knew, politicians, mighty CEOs; the architect wrote of things the men did to each other—things he had done—in the bathhouses. Much of it sickened me, the images that came to my head. I thought of the shapes of men roaming through cities, finding hidden rooms of bright, garish light.

"Doesn't hurt to hold onto these," my professor said, taking the bundle back from me when I had finished, folding them into their envelopes and tapping them efficiently together. She snapped a rubber band over them. "A woman never knows when this kind of evidence might come in handy."

Her lips formed an "O" then before each candle; she blew quickly, and ghosts of smoke rose in the darkness.

The next morning, sitting in my car in the rainy parking lot of the college, skipping an African Politics class, I kept seeing the professor organize those letters; it had stunned and quieted me, her pragmatic treatment of them. And I was baffled by the relationship between the professor and her husband. There was something about his intense confessions that made me imagine her making love to him—her face in practiced ecstasy. Was lovemaking part of her act, like the wearing of the dresses? Was it possible the architect had this disease that was killing people—and then perhaps did I?

There was a fog around the cars, the gates to the college paths; through my rain-soaked windshield now I watched the campus, students going in and out of the snack bar, and the ice-covered ivy buildings. College girls walked over the pathways in tight jeans, their hair a little iced, some holding umbrellas. I wanted to wake up in my apartment bedroom with one of them, with their uncomplicated warmth, with flesh smooth and casual and undemanding next to mine. I shook my head at how difficult everything had become. I considered things over and again. I would find some way to exit this thing with the professor; I would free myself from the situation.

By late evening, back in my room, I'd lost all resolve. I kept thinking of the professor's confident eyes, and the way she seemed to know and anticipate every dark impulse I had. I thought of her voice in my ear. My hunger, after our months of rough, easy sex, grew more fierce with each hour of absence.

She phoned as I was thinking it all through, as I was pacing the floor; it was as if she knew precisely when to contact me. Her husband had flown to a conference in Barcelona, she said; he would be there for the next week. I held the phone and looked out my window; I watched the lit, rain-sparkling back of Christ, the used car dealership across the intersection with its soaked, defeated flags.

"Don't think so much," she said. "Don't be so Goddamned heavy. Just come to me. I'll leave the door open."

I imagined the architect, then, standing at a podium, indicating with a pointer something on a precise, bright screen. I thought of him walking through a shadowed club in Spain, smiling at other men while here in dark, storming New England, his wife called me to her.

Soon enough my windshield wipers slapped at the rain. Streetlights looked like weeping, mourning stars. Hunched forms moved furtively on the sidewalks, ducking into alleys, some with umbrellas, some just with raincoats slung over them—a river of men looking for refuge. Building lights filtered onto the shining brick sidewalks.

The house was a black shape on the ridge, darker still without any moon. My Ford crackled into the driveway. No lights waited for me. I sensed that the professor felt the house lights would make me consider things—think—frighten me off. But my surrender was not in question. I shut off headlights, my engine; I sat a moment in the car, that complete ticking-car rain-drumming darkness around me. The front door of the house was ajar. I ran through the downpour, groped my way inside, went under the turning fans, up the stairs. I felt for the space of the professor's doorway. The storm was hitting the house in waves.

Now here she was, her naked weight pressing against me. Here were her lips, the warm, perfect curve of her back, the points of her eyes looking up, the sandalwood scent of her neck. The curtains were drawn and when we moved to the bed I was nearly blind, catching only the faintest, most immediate glances of our flesh: a hand, a thigh, a curve of hip—then the animal tightness of our connection. There were moments when, but for the physical sensations I experienced, we might not even have existed.

That rain came down hard, and outside there was the low roar of the river. Here, in this place—this ecstatic blackness—the professor and I twisted together in our familiar rage.

ROBERT ROBERT ROBERT

WHEN the mother comes back into the room after paying the babysitter, her son is still there on the couch, the back of his head and shoulders a silhouette against the bright television. He is four. It is Saturday, his night to stay up as late as he wishes. The woman's husband, the boy's father, dressed in evening clothes, sits in the easy chair to the side with his glasses on and a newspaper. He has loosened his tie. A small lamp lights the paper and his fingers.

Two hours ago, the woman's husband was charming at the restaurant, at the head of the table, thanking his managers for the year, the jump in sales. The firm rented an entire dining room, and from the fourteenth floor windows everyone could see sparkling Boston under rain. Waiters with wine bottles stood to the side until her husband's speech was finished, then moved forward to fill glasses. Candles made amber light in the wine. Voices rose with appreciation for her husband, a burst of applause for this recognition, this evening out. She, the wife, was charming too, her egalitarian hand on the forearms of other wives, leaning forward pleasantly to listen to other husbands, knowing that later these couples would discuss how successfully they had maneuvered themselves into her favor.

She and Robert drove home by the coast. They had operated smoothly together all night, but the act was done and there was no need to speak or fill the air with small talk. She watched his hands on the steering wheel, the cut of his jaw, steady adjustments of eye. It was fall and dark and storming and you could see the white of waves below the curving road, on the rocks.

Now the woman stands beside the modern rosewood table. She removes her earrings, tilting her head, and takes off her heels. She has given the babysitter a generous tip. She puts her thin purse into the top drawer of the table.

Rain dashes against the house, and the windows are dark and wet. The television light flickers over her son. The film is black and white; cars are going at that 1940s speed, a little too fast to be realistic. Orchestral notes fall dramatically. Inside a forbidding mansion, a man holds a gun up to another and fires. The second man sinks to the floor. He raises his hand, a last, feeble defense. The shooter stands above him with menace, and the brass of the orchestra moans with despair.

"Robert," her son says anxiously. "Robert. He's going to kill him."

The father puts down his newspaper and watches the television. His glasses reflect the advance of the shooter, the glint of the gun. He brings the newspaper up again.

The gunman grins. The orchestra builds to a crescendo. There *is* something terrible, the woman thinks, something awfully black, about the scene.

"Robert. *Robert*," the boy says. "Robert?"

"He's not going to kill him," his father says. "That's just acting."

The mother glares at her husband. She thinks, *Hell*. She steps forward and strokes her son's hair. "You don't need to see this, honey. We can turn it off if you want."

Her son looks at her with wet, unfocused eyes, then shakes his head *no* and turns back to the screen.

"It's a *mo*vie, Rebecca," her husband says, behind his paper. "Let's not make a federal case of it, all right?"

A detective steps through the doorway. He pulls his revolver and fires. The bad guy grimaces, holds his chest. Victorious music plays. A pretty woman comes into the room, her hands to her face, her dress impossibly pristine.

"There, see that?" the husband says, with the paper still in front of him. "All finished. Now let the kid watch his movie."

Oh Goddamn it to hell hell hell, the mother thinks. She removes her silver barrette and shakes her hair out angrily. She goes to the bathroom for aspirin. The light in there makes her head pound. The names of various products scream at her from the cabinet. She takes off her makeup and bathes her face in cool water, trying to concentrate on this tiny submergence and not on the faint, frantic sounds of machine guns and violins down the hall. She pats her face dry with a towel, and holds the cloth against her forehead with her eyes closed.

When she comes out again the actress, in another sweeping dress, is kissing the detective. They are on a veranda and fireworks are glittering high in the night sky. The actress has her hand on the back of the detective's neck, bringing him close. They move their heads around passionately.

"Robert," the boy says. "Robert. *Robert Robert Robert.* How come they're doing this?"

His father keeps on reading.

"Robert," the woman says, with a long, measured breath. "Our son is talking to you."

Her husband sighs and puts down his newspaper and looks at the television. His glasses are two infinitesimal screens, two small squares of kissing light. "That's what people do when they like each other," he says. "They're just kissing."

The boy stares at his father, a profile of curiosity that makes the woman suddenly, strangely dizzy. It is as if the house is rocking and falling beneath her. Her husband, taking off his glasses, looking at their boy, seems momentarily startled as well.

The woman watches the two of them as they turn back toward the screen. Her son's head is a steady silhouette again against the brightness. Her husband puts his glasses on and presses his lips together and, with a brusque shake, straightens out the crease in his paper and brings it up to read. She watches him wet the tip of a finger and prepare to turn the page.

THE GREAT WHITE BLUESMAN

—in the Merrimack Valley of Massachusetts: 1984

STU is blowin' on his harp and when I open my eyes all I can see at first is his curly brown hair and *his* eyes, green like mine, and his hands pressed against the microphone, which he keeps right up close to his mouth and his harp. He's wailin' his solo on *Blues With A Feeling,* which is slow and deep and pounds at you in your gut, and my Gibson is just keeping rhythm, *wop, boom boom, wop,* like that. I hardly hit chords on this one, as long as I'm keeping time.

It's the third set and my head is gone with eight Millers. I feel sweat on my arm and on the wood of my axe and coming down my forehead under my hair, and my eyes are closed and my fingers, *they* know what they're doing on the fretboard, even though I don't. Behind us, Jeezer on drums and Slick on bass are shaded, because they're playin' back, out of the cheap yellow lights they gave us tonight, and Slick in his scam Bogart hat nods at me, swaying, and there is nothing on his face, just, *yeah, man, let's make it through this set and go have some air and a smoke.* Jeezer is black and Slick is black and Puerto Rican, and when they're back out of the lights and keeping the pounding going I don't see much of them anyway. I *feel* them, though, they're right there, *wop, boom boom, wop,* deeper and crisper and more heavy than me. Stu finishes his solo and now Slick steps up, singing, and I squint through the lights and down by the bar these two guys are standing with drinks in their hands and behind one of them a long girl in a black dress and black hair with a red ribbon comes up. She rests her head on the shoulder of one of the guys and he looks surprised at his friend as if to say, all *right,* and she smiles

32

and her smile is nice and slow, and her hands snake around his neck and then back and under his arms and her fingernails are red and her fingers move on his chest and stomach with the music. She rubs her cheek on the man's neck and he's still looking like, *look what I found,* and his friend is laughing; *she's cocked,* the laughter says, *and you're lucky as hell she found you.*

Our parents saw that we were a problem when we were very young. "Jacob William Burke," my mother would say to me, "I don't know why I had the two of you. That Stuart is just the devil's edge, just a little worse than yourself." She was being funny when she said that, but neither she nor my Dad was funny when we threw pine cones across the road at cars two days before Halloween. "But Pop," we said, "they were only pine cones, not rocks or anything. And we were just practicing up for Halloween." That really got him mad. He was the chief of police in Methuen, and he'd chase kids all day and then he'd have to come home to us. I can remember being on the stairs and watching his back slumping in the kitchen as my mother would say, "There's a little bad news from school on our dynamic duo." "Oh, Jesus," he would say, "what have they done now?"

They sent us to a Catholic reform school when I was in fourth grade and Stu was in the sixth. But we filled Sister Selma's desk full of salamanders, frogs and toads, and she came in at Morning Grace and opened a drawer and a slimy frog leaped out and fell, sprawling, across her desk, and she shrieked and I had my face all scrunched up—trying not to laugh—and she turned white and looked at me and her face turned to stone, and she said, "Burke, come here."

We were out of St. Mary's in a year, then. Our eyes from the living room couch watched my father in his blue police trousers and t-shirt pacing up and down, swearing, saying, "I wonder who reformed who at that Goddamned school, because you two sure didn't change."

Outside the wind is swinging the sign that says *The Front Page.* The wind and the summer night wake me up a little and I don't feel so fucked-up anymore. We lean against the van, the "B-mobile," we call it, after our group, the B-Street Blues Band. Stu goes inside the van, saying, "I'm gonna change my fuckin' pants." "Why?" I say. "We're three sets in. Who gives a fuck?" But he's rustling inside the van and when he comes out he's pulled off his jeans and wears clean blue corduroys, and he says, "I felt like scum in those torn pants. Look at Jeezer, man. The pimp of B-Street." Jeezer's sort of the different one in the group. He only came to B-Street a year ago, when our old drummer left us. He wears good, clean clothes, and he's big, so on him the clothes look like they got a little class. White suits and shit, smooth tan pants. Sometimes on stage he wears a straw cowboy hat and calls himself "the Texas Nigger." The rest of us go with what we've got, which ain't much.

I ask Stu for a smoke and he says, "Fuck you, you owe me three already," which is true, I do. But Slick comes over, and I smell beer and smoke on him as he leans in, he's a little shorter than me, and he says, "Hey, man," up close, like black guys do, and he's holding a cigarette on my chest between his fingers. "Thanks, man," I say, "I owe you," and wonder as I say it when I can give him some smokes back.

We're playing in Lowell, and we talk about Kerouac and I say I just read *The Dharma Bums* and Stu says Dickens was here, once, and we all say, *No shit. So this has been the gutter for more than the likes of us.* The street is well-lit and the sidewalks are brick and cobblestone and the summer night air is smooth and nice to breathe. Across the street at The Derby I hear sounds of a rock band and see the windows full of light and shapes and colors like a moving watercolor painting. They offered us more money to play there once but we said no, 'cause The Derby's high class, snotty crowds and that's not us, we're just kick-ass blues. We're fine with what we make, and we dig Sam. Sam owns The Front Page and it's tight for him with the bucks but he always pays right after the show and he doesn't bullshit, which is better than you get in most places. He's fifty-five and plays the harmonica and sometimes we let him on stage with us. He loves Stu, because of how well Stu plays harp. He calls Stu his "best-behaved illegitimate son."

After Kerouac and Dickens we get heavy. I pull out some Wild

Irish Rose, which is kind of the B-Street trademark, and Slick shouts, "Wild I, Wild I!" Stu and Slick and I keep our backs against the van and pass the bottle and call ourselves derelicts and laugh, but Jeezer doesn't drink with us. He's sitting in the front seat and I see him when he bends forward and puts the small glass tube to his nose, and I think, *shit, if it's a fat line it'll keep him pounding the sticks good for the last set.*

Stu and me met Slick, alias Juan Torrez, in 1977. We dug Elvis and early Beatles and the Stones and Buddy Holly and Stu especially liked Paul Butterfield and Chicago-style blues. We were all just fucking around, then. We rented an old warehouse down where "B" street used to be, near the railroad tracks in Lawrence, where the mills are by the river. There was a liquor store a couple of blocks down from our place and pretty soon, on warm nights, all the winos were standing outside our door, listening to the blues. We didn't have a drummer then and I guess having a steady drummer has been a problem for us all along. We never had one stick with us for more than two years. But me and Slick and Stu were always the core of the thing, man. We were the band.

Sometimes we'd invite a wino in named Jimmy who hung around the area and dug blues. We'd let him in the warehouse when he wasn't fucked-up and wouldn't start shouting or acting crazy. He'd sit in a corner, near Slick, and I'd watch the old man listening to us and I remember how young his eyes looked, framed by the age of his face. Something in the music made his eyes that way. He'd stomp his feet and dip his head and shoulders with the beat, and run his hand across his scruffy beard.

Jimmy wasn't around the day we named the band. We were jamming in the warehouse. It was raining outside and the windows were streaked running-water gray from the rain and the dirt mixing and going down the glass in little rivers, and our guitar cases—which are black and covered with stickers—looked blue in the light. We were thinking about the famous nicknames performers have, like "Mississippi John Hurt" and "Screamin' Jay Hawkins," and Stu says, "I know what we'll name Juan. We'll call him Slick 'cause of his hair." Slick had his hair slicked back in those days, and he wore large black sunglasses like Ray Charles. "Yeah," Stu says, (he couldn't stop pressing), "we'll call him Slick the

Spick." Well, Slick didn't dig the "Spick" part much but the "Slick" stayed. Then they start thinking about me. I went through a host of names that day. "Honest Jake Burke," they called me for a while, then: "Humping Honest Able Jake," then—this was Stu's suggestion—"Humping Honest Able, The Great Fornicator, Liberator of all the whores on B-Street." I said it would take too long to say on stage, so Stu settled on "Smokin' Jake Burke." Slick named Stu "The Great White Bluesman," because, he said, it always surprised him when white boys played good blues.

We thought about what to call ourselves as a group, just in case we ever landed a drummer, and we sat there, quiet for a while, looking out at the street and the rain, at the telephone wires that sagged over the brick buildings and the river, and the spots and ripples on the water. It was Stu who looked at the sign, bent over a little at the end, that said "B-Street." "That's it," he said. "The B-Street Blues Band."

Before we were out of high school we had a drummer named Rich and we had already fronted the James Montgomery Blues Band and Cub Koda and a few other good, hard blues acts. We named Rich "Psycho" because he looked like Anthony Perkins in the movie. He got crabs once and we said, "Good, Psycho. You've been sleeping with a nice clean crowd."

***

Two weeks later, the summer season is ending and we're at our last good beach gig of the season, at Mr. Goodbar, in Old Orchard Beach, Maine. Stu's singing *The Wanderer,* doing a hell of a job of it— he sounds just like a young Goddamn Dion—and when we hit the last few notes the room explodes in applause and Stu's saying, into the microphone, "Thank you very much, ladies and gents, it's been a real pleasure. This is a tune we'd like to end on, we wrote it ourselves, Slick and I did. It's called *The Lawrence Nocturne,* and we hope you'll dig it—" and the crowded dance floor yells and whoops and Jeezer tips back his cowboy hat and his sticks hit the drums and we're into it. We've got a big crowd and they've been dancing all night and I've been watching a girl with curly blond hair and nice, large firm jugs that shake when she dances. Her neck is wet and she *moves,* man, while a lot of dancers just pretend. Her whole body curves and flexes and her head goes back and forth with the rhythm and I'm watching that golden hair against a slate blue dress and white teeth and deeply tanned skin. Stu sees me watching and shouts in my ear, "Don't jack off onstage. It's offending to the management." I nod and smile and go into the first solo and hope maybe she'll notice me. Then, as I play, I'm remembering a high school dance when Stu asked Stephanie Haberstane to dance with him. This chick was sort of the hit one of the school and Stu was known as a wildman, and he comes stepping up and says, "Hey, man, you wanna dance?" Stephanie and her friends looked at him like he was a bug, and Stephanie said, firmly, "No." But Stu stared back at her, deadpan, and said, good and loud, "So I guess a blow job's out of the question then, huh?"

I laugh and fuck up the solo but nobody notices and Stu sees me laughing and he laughs too, even though he doesn't know what it's all about. Then he jumps into his solo and I watch him, and suddenly Blondie in front of me is just another one to watch, just another one I've seen.

Afterwards, Blondie has left, I don't see her anywhere, and the bouncer is trying to make everyone leave, saying, "Listen man, I don't want to break up the party but we're already past closing time," and Slick and I are sitting at a table and Slick is having a smoke. I have two empty beer bottles in front of me and I'm on my third. I'm looking around the room and I can't see Stu or Jeezer.

"Where's Stu?"

"I don't know," Slick says. "I think they're in the dressing room. Jeezer had some coke he wanted to lay on Stu."

"No shit," I say. "I'm drivin'."

Slick laughs. "Don't make no fuckin' difference, does it? Not one of us is going to hold it straight on the road anyway. You and your fuckin' Wild I and beers. But you're probably right, maybe you and I oughtta take turns."

We keep on laughing, joking, talking about which of the girls we'd like to do tonight and how. I mention Blondie. The bouncer is gently shoving a small man in a red and black lumber shirt who keeps saying, "you asshole, you asshole," like to nobody at all. The bouncer smiles at us as if to say, *I don't know where they come from.* The more people clear out, the more the place looks dead. Beer bottles and cigarettes are everywhere, and the waitresses, all worn-out looking with frizzy hair and sweat circles under their arms, are pushing together as many bottles as they can hold, and the bottles go *clink, clink* as the girls bundle them in their arms, then *chunk* and a high-pitched *crash* as they are tossed into plastic barrels. Above, the smoke has collected on the ceiling and made the yellow lights dim.

We load speakers and monitors and our guitars and the drums into the back of the B'mobile, 'cause this is our last night of three at Mr. Goodbar. Stu and Jeezer sit in the back, on the equipment, and I can see, looking there from the rear view mirror, that Stu's eyes are racing, watching the lights outside the van. Old Orchard Beach is a resort town, with an amusement park and a lot of honky-tonk stores. It's two in the morning and even though you can't see the ocean in the darkness you can feel it, raw and soggy on you, in you, and smell it, fresh and salty. I'm shaking my head to get things clear, but the orange and red lights outside—what's left of them at this hour of the morning—don't get clear for me. There's a fog coming in from the sea, which doesn't help much. I hear Slick's voice beside me asking if I'm okay and I say yeah, yeah, and in the mirror Jeezer is watching two black guys stumble down the sidewalk and he says, "What do ya know? They got niggers in Maine." Stu laughs hysterically, and I feel like saying, *Will you two shut up? It's hard enough without you fuckers giggling like girls,* but I don't say anything, because I know it's me, in my head, not them, and I concentrate and by the time we've made it through the back roads to 95 South the fog has settled in thicker, *pea soup, my father used to call it,* but I know I'll be all right, I can feel it, in my chest, a hollow, hungry feeling that says I'm tired but I'll stay awake.

Ahead in the fog as I drive, a green wall is in front of me. It looks like vapor and then a green ghost and then a bridge as the van goes *whoosh* underneath and through.

***

In September, all of the blues groups in Lawrence get together for a show called "Blues Fusion." The groups each do a half-hour set, then get together at the end of the evening, call ourselves "Fusion," and play one hour of the best blues and funk this side of Boston.

All of us who play in Fusion are old friends. A lot of us have covered in each other's bands when someone was sick or couldn't make it. The audience knows us personally—they've stayed with us through the years. So Blues Fusion is like a reunion, like one big party where we play good music and see old friends and get stoned.

We rehearsed three days for the show and now the rehearsing was over and I came back to my apartment and opened a Miller and turned on channel 56 to *The Three Stooges*. I have a poster of them on one wall. I hadn't drunk much through the evening so I was still pretty straight but my head felt dull. I could hear the drums clicking in my brain and I realized I had a headache so I went to the bathroom, got three aspirins, and popped them down with my Miller. Then I drank another one and went to bed.

My mattress and box spring sit on the floor and when I lie down and look out the window I see the top of a chimney and the night sky when my light is out. I spent a long time with my arms folded behind my head on the pillow, looking out at the dark, listening: I had my window open. Cars were stopping and starting below, and at the steps of the church across the intersection I could hear the kids speaking Spanish and laughing and once a bottle smashed. Then the rain came, tapping softly at first on the screen, and later harder as the wind blew, and I got up and shut the window a little. There was no one around the church anymore.

By the time I start getting nervous it's 10:10 and we'll be going on in twenty minutes. The Knights of Columbus building is jammed on the

39

main floor: the crowd of five hundred sits at tables, dances, or stands on chairs at the back. Slick and me are in a corner of the bar, watching the show through a large connecting window where people are pressed up close, ordering drinks, waving bills, swaying with the music of the Bombers, who behind them are playing a slow rhythm and blues tune. I see the lead singer from my angle: he's stocky and dressed in black leather and he has black curly hair and the blue light is on him. Below him, standing against the stage with a jam of other people, a woman reaches out and puts a hand on the singer's shin, and he smiles at her, then leans back his head and body as he hits a high part of the song. I see sweat on a bartender's forehead as he tries to keep up with orders coming from the bar and the floor. Slick and I drink Grand Dads and I'm feeling good because we lit up a joint in the parking lot a while ago, and Slick and I have been drinking a couple of bottles of Blue Nun through the afternoon.

The emcee of the show, James Agar, who owns the "Head's Up" shop on Broadway, comes walking up and lays a hand on Slick's shoulder. He's dressed in glitter rock clothes from his shop and Elton John sunglasses, and he turns around to show us his shirt, advertising his store, that says, *Good Head: 215 Broadway.* We laugh and his pale, washed-out face grins along.

"You dig?"

"We dig, bro," Slick says.

"You guys ready to go on?"

"Fucked-up and ready," I say.

"Good, good," Agar says, and spins us around, and puts a hand on both our shoulders and leads us through the lobby, by the cops, onto the floor. The music is loud here and he has to shout in my ear.

"Where's Stu and Jeezer?"

"I saw them an hour ago," I yell. "They'll be here. They're comin', man." We push our way through people and I feel nice as I slide by smooth, female ass, some of them dressed to the nines. A few of the people clap us on the backs and say hello, and we say hello, hello, and smile.

We make it to the clear space on the far side of the stage where the roadies stand in bored positions or sit on the equipment boxes. The Bombers are into their last song and the drums are beating hard. Stu and Jeezer make it here too, from another side of the room, they're both sweating, they've been fighting to get through the dancers. The floor, with all those people, is hot and wet. Slick leans over to Agar's ear and shouts, "Can we go on now? I think I'm peaking." Agar laughs and says "Yeah," just as the Bombers song ends and the lights go black and pandemonium takes over. In the darkness Agar leaves us to go onstage and I feel Stu and Jeezer and Slick close to me, and their nerves, tight: but we are one, standing there, and it eases the pain.

A white light hits Agar and another cheer rises from the crowd and he holds out his arms to silence them and his arms sparkle with the glitter.

"Ladies and gents," he says, in a gutsy, Wolfman-Jack voice, "now I've got the group you've all waited to see—" (some of the crowd in the back starts shouting "B-Street, B-Street ...") "—these are the meanest cats comin' outta Lawrence, the meanest cats comin' outta anywhere. This band's played with James Montgomery (cheering, whistling), they've played with my man, Cub Koda (cheers, whistling, applause), and last night they played with some of the *ugliest* women I have *seeeen* in my life. (Laughter, more whistling.) Ladies and gents (we start walking onstage), I give you (he points at us)—the B-Street Blues Band!"

As the lights hit us I can't see anything but the faces near the stage: my hands are sweating, and my ears just hear noise, the clapping and whistling and shouting and Jeezer hitting a couple of drums like he always does before we start playing. I find my Gibson and amp and plug in the jack, thinking hard about my first chord, because I have to start out the first number, *Bandit of Love*, a Bohumin tune. The lights go from white to blue and I see Stu's hand in the air, counting out, *a one, two, a one, two, three four*—and my fingers hit the lead and it is solid and the drums and bass hit, and Stu starts singing:

41

I got some names in a little black book
You don't believe me you just take a look
You had your time but your time is up
Well I guess you don't go messin' with the Bandit of Love—

I'm looking at Stu and for the first time tonight I really watch him. He's got sweat all over his forehead and his eyes aren't like they usually are, closed through the first song, they're looking quickly at the lights and the people, down and up, nervous, and I remember those eyes that night in Maine, how they didn't look at me, but at the lights outside the van, how they raced that same way.

You run around and you make me so blue
But listen here honey I can run around too
You had my heart but my heart is done—
Well I guess you don't go messin' with the Bandit of Love

The crowd moves in front of us, a hundred heads across the stage move in rhythm, side to side, back, they dig our beat and we can feel it. Behind them, the blackness moves, too, I can only see a few people in back at the main doorways, but I can *feel* the room around us moving. It's about now we start to leave the nervousness behind and switch into automatic, letting the music take over, but I can't do it somehow, watching Stu. His eyes are moving faster, he's sweating more, and he's having trouble with the words, like his voice is catching as he breathes.

Bandit of Love—I'm breakin' so free
Cuz' your little finger ain't no place to be
You had your time but your time is up—
Well I guess you don't go messin' with the Bandit of Love

As I go into the last solo Stu grabs the mike stand and just stands there, not moving to the beat, not moving at all, and he closes his eyes and in the light I see the sweat shining on the side of his face and matting his hair. His chest starts heaving, up and down, and he tilts his head back. I stop in the middle of the solo and the bass and drums keep going and as I walk over, I forget about my amp and the jack rips out of it but I don't give a shit. Slick stops playing and the crowd in front of us becomes disjointed, like one large black animal falling to pieces. Stu is shaking his head and then he falls, heavy, and the microphone booms and clatters like thunder as it hits the stage, and the light man gets wise, and flips out the lights.

Then everything goes fuckin' haywire. The people crowded up close to the stage start pouring over onto the boards, onto Stu, trying to pull him up, make him move, help him. But they're all drunk and as I set down my axe and throw microphones and amps and stoned, wasted people out of my way to get to Stu, I know that I'm gone too. My head isn't making any fucking sense and it's telling me *just get near him, get near him,* and around me is breathing, shouting, screaming everywhere and I'm on top of Stu, my arms straight, my hands on either side of his shoulders, I'm saying, "Fuckin' Stu, Fuckin' *Stu,*" and his eyes are frightened and he's breathing fast. People keep crowding in and I'm standing and hitting, swinging, I don't feel nothin' on my hands, just my head and mouth saying, "Get away, get away, you fuckin' vultures, get the fuck away," and I can feel water in my eyes because now Stu is drifting, down there on the dark, gritty stage boards beneath me, and then his eyes close while his head rolls, side to side. My stomach starts turning and I'm looking for somewhere, anywhere, to let it out, but I don't want to leave Stu.

It's Slick who finally pulls me away as the room lights are flipped on, and now while I blink and say, "Fuck you, I'm stayin'," I'm seeing the medics coming through the people, and the police pushing back the crowd, and one of the medics, stepping up, bending over Stu, is shouting, "We've got a coma," and then Stu disappears behind light blue shirts. Slick is saying, "It's better, bro. We have to get out of the way. We're no good the way we fuckin' are, anyway." Slick's arm is around my shoulders and he leads me down the stairs saying, "They were freebasing, man. It was no fuckin' good. No fuckin' good." I look around for Jeezer but he's nowhere that I can see, he's probably split, and suddenly I want to find him and hit him and hit him and say, *you bastard, for what you did to my brother, you fuckin' bastard* ... and while I'm hot and breathing hard I feel Slick's arm, muscular, around my back and up and his hand around the side of my neck holding me tight to him. "Walk, walk," he's saying.

He talks to me and leads me to a side door, and as we walk I look back through a gap in the medics around Stu. They're putting a tube in his arm and another in his nose and I say to Slick, "What the fuck are they doing to him?" and Slick just keeps saying, "Walk, man, walk. We need outside. We need air." I'm hearing his voice and the sounds around me like long distance, like when you have a bad head cold and it sounds like the world is outside your head and you've got your own world of echoes inside.

Then I hear rushing, pushing noises and they're taking Stu away and the tubes shiver around him and the hanging bottle rattles and I can just see his curly hair and his face, pale, eyes shut, against white sheets. The police clear a path, holding back people, and all I can think of is *Jesus, people look gray under normal house lights,* and I'm angry because my insides say I should be doing more for Stu but I can't think regular, all I can do is feel my eyes wet and watch as the glass doors close behind the medics and I see them hunch in the rain; then the siren is on and the path cleared of people fills again, as they look out the doors. Some of them are very drunk and a few of them laugh.

Outside I smell the rain on the tar. It rains so hard I hear it running fast in the gutters and splashing on the ground, and I tell Slick I want to go to the hospital and he says he'll drive. When I look through the rain into the night, I see the abandoned factory buildings across Marston Street, and a smokestack that rises solid black against the darkness. We reach the van and I wait with my hand tense on the wet door handle until Slick opens it from inside.

THE ANGRY BOY

WHEN he is eight, Jediah goes to the sea with his father. They drive a Buick and pull a sailboat behind on a trailer, and when they reach Beverly harbor Jediah stands on the tar at the water's edge, his hands in his pockets, watching his father's eyes narrow in the mirror as the wheels of the trailer crunch over ground and then wash and blacken through water. Soon the boat is nearly afloat; it is an O'Day *Flying Saucer,* a fast boat, and Jediah helps step the mast and fasten the stays. When the boat floats free of the trailer Jediah holds onto it by the front cleat, knee-deep in ocean water, the boom swinging idly behind him with the flapping mainsail. His father parks the car. His father is an old Navy man, an engineer who works at Futuraglass Yachtyards in Marblehead, and, as they sail, the bow pointing toward the Misery and Baker islands, Jediah feels his father's assurance throughout the craft: the tightness of sails in steady wind, the waves singing on the fiberglass hull, and the bow-wave hissing. There are brown horizons of islands before them, and the blue of sea stretching away, and to the side houses dot the shore of the mainland, neatly tucked into folds of hills and trees. It is a warm, white and blue day, and biplanes fly from Beverly airport over the harbor, trailing long advertisements behind. *Magic Show—Beverly Theatre Tonight—One Nite Only,* they say, or *Barley Auto—Rts 128 and 97.* Now the *Flying Saucer* sails past the large black sign, propped on a pillar of stones, with man-sized white letters: 5 MPH. Jediah looks at the rush of white water on the rocks, sparkling suddenly with sun, and the seaweed floating on the waves. Then, when they are past the harbor, he believes he can see deeply into the ocean, shafts of sun-

45

light glancing off creatures below: flounder he and his father have fished for off Baker Island, sand sharks and fiddler crabs they have seen in the shallows.

"Dad?"

"H'm?"

"Will you die before I die?"

"I think so."

"Do you have to?"

"I think so."

"I don't want you to."

His father's hand is large on the tiller, and Jediah looks up at the wind-tightened gray eyes. The hand pulls up on the mainsail sheet, lets it out until the sail receives a new bite of wind. "Then I won't," his father says. "Then I won't die before you do. I'll make sure we stay together."

"That's good," Jediah says. "That's how I want it." He turns, listens to the water rushing as the boat picks up speed.

"We'll get drinks and fries at McDonald's after," his father says, smiling, louder now. Jediah sees these words as pictures in his sun-warmed, closed eyes: golden arches by the harbor, the pier looking over the forest of masts and marina buildings, the gulls calling and whirling in the air above, and he and his father tossing fries up into the sky and watching the birds snatch them from gravity.

At night, before sleep, Jediah's father reads to him from *20,000 Leagues Under The Sea*. He lays in the crook of his father's heavy arm and chest, listening to evening: crickets peeping in the yard, the stream gurgling and deep chants of bullfrogs beyond, his mother's low humming from the next room as she irons. Jediah sees all of these things as images, transported there by their sounds, in the same way his father's voice brings him into Captain Nemo's parlor, where he starts a tour of the splendid *Nautilus*. There, before him, the captain's hand points to a place beyond the giant glass porthole, at the world of colorful fish gliding by and sunken galleons strewn

46

across the ocean floor. Now, his dream following the rise and fall of his father's voice, he is walking with the Captain and Conseil and Ned Land through an underwater forest by the island of Crespo, and they dive together for cover behind sea coral and plants to avoid two "monstrous" sharks that flow with the current above them, *"horrible creatures which could crush a man with their cruel jaws!"*

On August days Jediah and Steve Young ride to the Village Store and buy comic books with their allowances. Jediah buys the pulpy episodes of *Voyage To The Bottom Of The Sea,* about the adventures of a submarine crew far beneath the surface of the ocean. They come home from the warm, orange and green-dappled road, leaning their bikes against the side of the garage, and go down into the cool cement basement. There, they play submarine: the workbench transforms into a control center, and the high window looking out to green leafy plants becomes a porthole staring at the underwater world. The periscope they use is purely pretend: they activate it downward and unsnap the handles and lean against it with head and elbows as expertly as if it were there, then snap the handles and send it smoothly up, into the hull, their hands making steady motions through the air. Jediah can hear the pulse of sonar in his head, and he plays the part of a stunned captain as the whale hits them and he and Steve reel from wall to wall, a sidelong stumbling of shoulders into cement, thankful for their amazingly durable vessel.

On a warm afternoon, reading *Voyage To The Bottom Of The Sea* in the front yard hammock, Jediah comes upon an advertisement. None of the other ads, of musclemen and ray guns, attract him, but this one does. It is a picture of a small submarine, with a section of the side cut away so that you can see a boy, about Jediah's age, happily manning the brightly-winking controls. *Own Your Own Submarine!* the advertisement says. *$17.95, While They Last!* Jediah reads about the underwater world available to him, and his hands clutch the sides of the magazine tightly. He sees himself in the submarine, imagines Steve's admiring eyes on that day of the maiden voyage in Baldpate Pond. *Can I drive it?* Steve would say. *Well, maybe after a while,* Jediah would say, because he would want to be at the controls, watching the underwater world unfold before him. He *would* let Steve drive it, he decided now as he was thinking feverishly of all this, because he was always generous with his things. And what would be deep in the pond where he spent his summer days swimming? The rainbow trout and pickerel he and his father fished for, certainly, and the stone wall that ran through the area of the pond where once, long ago, there had been a cow pasture. And bottles, probably, and old boats. But wouldn't it be exciting, that first time, to submerge beneath the waves!

Jediah leaves the hammock swinging, runs through the house, past his startled mother in the kitchen and up to the coolness of his room, to his desk. He pushes aside models of the USS *Nautilus* and USS *Triton,* and dumps quarters from his allowance bottle. He takes paper and a pencil and counts, from time to time smelling the metallic smells of the coins and then touching them gently, like gifts: five dollars and twenty-five cents. He subtracts—and he is down to twenty-four weeks he will still have to save. Twenty-four weeks! For a while, he sits at the desk, staring at his hands and the small pilings of coins. Then he walks downstairs, and asks his mother if, for more errands, he can have an increase in allowance.

She will let him weed the garden and the sides of the driveway, and his allowance is raised from fifty cents to one dollar a week. And she calls her neighbor, Mrs. Knotts, who, for eight dollars, will let Jediah paint the trimming of a window and stack wood. "It's for something *special,*" Jediah's mother says, smiling into the phone. "He won't tell me what." That night, after dinner, Jediah sits in the stairwell, reading *Voyage To The Bottom Of The Sea,* and overhears his mother proudly telling his father, "He says it's for something *special,*" and his parents laugh together. Jediah keeps himself from blushing by turning to the advertisement and reminding himself that it is, indeed, for something special.

He has to remind himself of that often, as he bends to the gnarled weeds in the driveway, the sun on his back and shoulders and neck

48

and his hands grasping at roots, then digging and overturning dirt with the spade, as his mother showed him. And then on walks from the Knotts' forest, from the block where Mr. Knotts has split wood to the side of the garage, where Jediah makes a neat stack. His arms smell of earth and bark and his shoulders are tired and strained. And later he holds the paintbrush over the windowpane in the porch of the Knotts' house, the bristles pressing against wood and tape, laying a smooth layer of gray on the new trimming. Jediah carefully removes the tape when he finishes, and examines his work. His arms hurt from the lifting, and he has a headache from the oil smell of the paint, but the work has not bothered him. It is only the thought of other children in their submarines, gliding through the underwater worlds of all the lakes in America, that has worried him, because that phrase in the advertisement has stayed with him: *While They Last.* He goes to the door and knocks, and asks Mrs. Knotts for aspirin and his eight dollars. She takes him inside and sits him in the house, cool laundry and fabric smells, and returns with a glass of lemonade, and aspirin, and a crisp ten-dollar bill. His eyes widen and he thanks her and drinks lemonade and walks home whistling and touching the bill, thinking of two weeks saved.

When he has earned the money at last, he takes the ten-dollar bill from Mrs. Knotts, the five he has exchanged with his father for quarters, and three crumpled one-dollar bills, and puts them in a brown envelope along with the cut-out advertisement with his name and address. He rides to the Village Store and buys two six-cent stamps, then puts the envelope into the mailbox outside, feeling as it slides in three weeks of his life going into that box, and a dream. Then he rides home.

***

Now it is late August, and the summer light falls earlier. Jediah walks on a path he and his friends have made to the stream, and watches the sun filter through trees on a far hill, through clear water: it flows

49

over pebbles and jammed branches and weeds that undulate with the current. He waits there until his mother's voice, calling him to dinner, takes him from thoughts of his submarine, and he walks back through the darkening forest.

During the day, he rides to Baldpate pond with Steve, and they jackknife each other from the raft, Jediah springing from the diving board, feeling the lift of his body, turning back: sky, green water to the pines, stomach lifting, his hands clutching one knee. Then the plunge of water around him—the screaming voices at once become soft, insistent music underwater. He glances about at the pale shapes of other children—legs churning, arms treading; he lets himself sink beneath them until he can see their bodies above and shafts of sunlight and the dark shape of the raft and the chain trailing down to him in a lazy arc. *They are meant to be up there,* he thinks. *But this is where I am supposed to be.* Each day he rides home, he believes that he will see a large truck in his driveway with his submarine, and his mother will be talking excitedly with the truck drivers as they unload the vessel.

And then one morning, a Friday morning in the first week of September, Jediah's father is building shelves in the garage, and Jediah is handing him nails and holding boards as his father cuts them with the electric saw. Jediah's hands quiver with the wood and his ears ring in the air of shrill vibration. A UPS truck comes up the driveway and the saw whines and then dies, and Jediah and his father walk out into the sunlight. The driver takes out a one-by-three foot package and places it on the ground. He smiles at Jediah's father, holds out a clipboard and a pen. "Package for you, sir," he says.

Jediah's father takes the clipboard, reads, frowns. "It's for *you,* son," he says. He hands Jediah the pen and clipboard, and Jediah, confused, has to wait until the UPS man shows him where to scrawl his name. The man puts the pen behind his ear, winks, and climbs back into his truck. As the truck rolls to the road and away, Jediah stares at the box.

His father pulls out a knife and helps him open it. Inside, there is a note on top of a neat stack of cardboard pieces. The note says: *We are sorry to tell you we are out of submarines. We hope you are satisfied with your PATTON TANK. Best regards.*

Jediah feels his father's hand briefly on his shoulder, then hears the clanking of tools behind him. He takes the box to the yard, and dumps the pieces. Carefully, following directions, he puts the pieces together until what he has is another cardboard box, with green dots to indicate camouflage, and a plastic periscope punched through the top. He climbs under and sits inside the box, hearing his own breathing, and the sound the wind makes through the pines. Once he looks through the periscope, which weakly magnifies the stone wall at the start of the driveway. He stays in the dark place for a long time, smelling earth and cardboard.

Then, suddenly, he rises and throws the box away from him. He runs and kicks it, making it sprawl awkwardly across the yard. He tears at the cardboard, ripping the corrugated material into jagged pieces, making low sounds in his throat. He stamps at paper and dirt and grass until he is sweating and out of breath and pieces of green dotted cardboard and smashed plastic are scattered everywhere, cardboard dust swirling in the sun. Then he stands, breathing hard, his fists tight, looking at what his anger has done.

Later that evening, when his father and mother are reading by a fire in the living room, Jediah goes to the garage and turns on the light switch. He walks through smells of cement and oil and sawdust, turning over scraps of boards, looking at them closely. He takes a hammer and a box of nails from one of the shelves and goes outside, beneath the outdoor floodlight, and there he starts to work. In the woods the September cicadas are sawing, and far off the Knotts' dog begins his nightly howling. But Jediah does not hear these things. He places board on top of board, holds nails carefully, so that he can bring his fingers away quickly if he misses with the hammer, and strikes, once hitting his thumb, many times sending nails skittering with a silvery flash into the shadows of bushes. Once his father comes to the door, and watches quietly, and goes back inside. Jediah works until he feels empty in his chest and his cheeks are hot and his eyes are heavy. He gets up early and continues the next morning, and, by the time the sun is fully in the sky, he has something that looks like a large skateboard: there is a nose, and a body, and a small chair fashioned of two-by-fours. He pounds one nail into the front of the craft, bends it over, and using it as a hook, ties a rope to it and drags his submarine to the stream, grass brushing at his ankles as he pulls against the weight. The sun winks through the trees now as Jediah slides his boat into the slow-moving water. When he climbs aboard and sits in the seat, his construction wallows a moment and starts to sink. He catches his breath at the cool water soaking over his pant-legs and waist, and the bottom of his ship scrapes pebbles. He gets up, water streaming from him, steps to shore. His submarine, carried by the slight current, goes slowly downstream and lodges against a log. Jediah does not want to free it, or move it. He stands in his wet pants and shirt, shivering in the wind that is cool now with a hint of winter. Behind him, the steady sound of his father's hammer begins. He looks at the ripples the breeze makes on the stream, then turns and walks back through the morning forest to his home.

HER LOVER

AT the harborside candle and gift store, a place that smelled of paraffin and shellac and cinnamon, the woman said, "We can buy thirty-seven candles. The bathroom is full of mirrors. We'll put them in there and light them—" here she glanced about, lowered her voice conspiratorially, and leaned toward the man's ear, "—we'll make love there, like in a sea of a thousand candles."

She touched his chest with the pad of a forefinger. Her dark eyes were bright. She kissed him and turned, and began choosing candles from the rack on the wall: there were thin, tall white ones, and thicker, colored ones, some scented with black cherry, or lavender, or French vanilla. Soon she had a fistful.

The man, standing close behind her, smelled the candles and her perfume. Her scent made him think of their hotel room: he had arrived there before her last night and had watched through the large window as she'd come into the parking lot. She had been driving a sports car she'd rented at the airport. He remembered the fierce pull of her flesh almost immediately afterward, and how she had been naked on the bed when they'd finished, when they were laughing. He'd thought then, looking at her unguarded nakedness, that he might possibly love her. This had alarmed him, and he had tried to keep it from his face as she'd thrown her head back onto the pillow and laughed and he had watched her lovely throat move.

Her husband had called a few minutes later, phoning from their home in Arizona. He'd been on business in Europe and had just gotten the message that she would be working in New England when he returned. She had moved easily into their conversation. "*Thank* you, darling," she'd said. "It's hard to believe, another year. Holy shit, huh? I don't want to count them anymore."

The man, the lover, had tried to be as quiet on the bed as possible during the phone call, and had even worked to control his breathing. His silence had not simply been protective, but a moment of some shame, he'd realized, staring down at his hands, his legs, his feet. His thighs still had twitched uncontrollably with aftershocks of muscle and nerve. He'd looked up and watched the beautiful woman listening to the small, low voice on the receiver. Her husband had gone on and on. Once, she'd glanced over and rolled her eyes, and teased her lover with her bare foot. Then she'd turned away so that her lover could not see her face and said, quietly, "I love you too, darling."

Here in the candle store the man thought again about his breathing. He inhaled and exhaled carefully, the same way had last night on the bed. He felt as if any great intake of air, any indulgent liberty, might finish him off.

"Honey," he said. "I've got to go over those papers I told you about tonight."

Her back was to him, as she examined a candle in her free hand, but he could feel her collect herself and fold down like a map, preparing.

He said, "I know you're only here a short time, but that's the one thing I've got to do and I'd better get it done tonight."

She put down the candles and walked right out the door. He followed behind, feeling like an errant, stupid schoolboy. Outside, everything was bright and made him squint and the seaport was full of tourists. Banners of red, white and blue hung from the building eaves. A child near them was wrenching in its mothers' arms and saying *I want it I really really want it* and the mother was saying, *All right all right all right.*

"Christ, honey," he said, catching up.

"Forget it," she said, keeping to her hard clip and not looking at him. He could see a line of wetness from the corner of her eye to her tight jawbone. "You told me about the work. I knew about that.

Never mind."

They got into the man's car down the block and drove a mile to the neighboring island. This had been their plan after strolling about the seaport. Soon there were no more quaint shops, and a few simple bait shacks punctuated the highway, looking like they'd grown up from the sand. The sky was strikingly bright and open and the man's head began to ache. He could feel the woman's dark consideration of a small airport they passed; airplanes were tethered to the ground there in neat formation, and a windsock, stationary, rose over the runway. An airplane was taking off. It seemed to run parallel to them and then it was ahead and very suddenly, it lost the roughness of the earth and was rising, and the man could see the wings glint in the sun as the plane climbed and tilted south.

They went over a bridge where a sign welcomed them to the island. When they parked a block later the woman got out of the car and walked down the beach to the sea. She had lived in the southwest all of her life, she'd told him when she'd met him, in an Indianapolis convention center three months ago, and she had never seen the Atlantic ocean. In his hotel room that same night, after making love, she'd clutched him hard and bitten his chest and told him she wanted to be with him at the sea.

He followed behind her at about twenty paces. The ocean, too, seemed to be breathing carefully, the waves hissing as they came across the shore. The woman knelt on a dune above the water and her figure made a small shadow on the sand.

I've never seen the Atlantic ocean, she'd said. *I want to see the ocean with you,* she'd said. He imagined a thousand candle flames shifting to the wind of their flesh, and he knew that tonight he would see those flames in flickering multiplicity. *We'll make love,* she'd said. He could imagine the golden sweat at the base of her neck and the candles burning: halos of tentative fire in those mirrors, surrounding his many, open-mouthed faces of ecstasy.

THE CANDIDATE

THROUGH thunderous applause the candidate steps away from the podium, waving. He points to some campaign workers he recognizes; he shakes hands firmly. He thinks of how this will look on television. He gives a thumbs-up, pumps both arms.

He moves down, into the crowd. His campaign manager is touching his sleeve. She hands him a key. They have done this many times, in many different cities, but still her eyes fall a moment. She says, into his ear, *You'll need to be at the Civic Center in five hours. Seven o'clock. Will you make it?* The candidate nods. *Do you have your cell phone?* she says. *The directions?* He is nodding, looking at the lapel of her coat, the American flag pin there. Other voices pull at him, but he concentrates, slips the key into his pocket. *I'll ring once in case you're sleeping,* his campaign manager says.

They are in a university theatre. A curl of seats is above him: people stand, holding coats, watching. Blue carpet is beneath his feet. A college girl is here, grasping his fingers, anxious for this proximity to power. Here is a man with glasses and whiskers, making a point with earnest, desperate eyes; here an older woman with dyed, very black hair clapping the candidate's shoulder. The voices swell, signs and buttons are everywhere—the candidate's name in bold red and blue, white stars following. Microphone booms sway overhead; cameras fix on him. He is, suddenly and unexpectedly, the front-runner in the primary, with twenty-eight days to go. Flashbulbs explode, a sea of fragmented white.

He makes the trip in a rental car over the twisting New Hampshire highway, black oak trees bracing the empty sky. Where the road straightens he looks in the rearview mirror, and no cars are there, no reporters following. The tar is a gray stretch, bending into pines, the curve of a mountain.

He imagines his lover, the prostitute, hovering over Manchester, the Merrimack River winding below. In his mind now her feet touch down onto the airport ramp. She wears mules, jeans and sweater, her black sailor's jacket. Her hair is like combed wheat against it. She totes a small rolling suitcase. A limousine is waiting for her. She will arrive a little later than him.

When he eases into the hotel parking lot he looks around carefully. The route to his room is a set of open stairs to his left. He cuts the engine. He takes out the hotel key, throws a hooded jacket over his head and, hiding his face, sneaks to the stairway like a criminal.

He showers and is in a hotel bathrobe when the prostitute comes through the door. She has an extraordinary face: green eyes that sometimes are the color of a sunlit sea. The straight, wheat-blond hair falls over her cheek as she parks the rolling suitcase, removes her coat. Then she is in his arms, kissing his lips, his neck. She smells of jasmine: it is, to him, the smell of California—her home—a place where he will wage a final battle.

They sit on the bed, on a neat, cotton-ribbed blanket. She holds his hands, squeezes them sometimes for emphasis. *The flight was fine,* she says, *thank you;* she has been in Buenos Aires, she has danced nights at clubs with porteñas whose faces are flushed with Spanish-Italian blood. The city never sleeps. The other night she was on the plaza, where there is a statue of José de San Martin. He was their Bolívar. *I thought of you,* she says.

The candidate shows her the newspaper that was in the room when he came. *I think I look exhausted,* he says. She leans over to look at the photograph. *Gravity is making me look like some naked opportunist,* he says.

She brings his hands up and kisses them; she looks at his eyes. She says, *You're doing so well. I've been watching it on C-SPAN. You're going to win this.* She grasps the hair of his chest beneath his bathrobe and tugs until he laughs. *I'm going to shower, honey,* she says. *You'd better be a naked opportunist when I get back.*

She studies sociology at UCLA, is working on a doctorate in political science. She is twenty-seven. He has been meeting her for ten months. She will be with him again, next week, in Iowa, and then very soon after that in South Carolina. He imagines the southern hotel, white waves on a winter beach, the cold, bright smell of the salt. She is his oasis.

Across the room the door is slightly ajar, and he hears the spin of her body beneath water, the spray lapsing, then drumming. The glazed oak trees outside, the main street buildings, take on a hopeful light for a moment. The sky is bright slate blue, the ice of the balcony railing is burning. Then everything suddenly darkens, as if someone has turned down a great dimmer light. Snow drifts in the air. The candidate sits on the bed and thinks that death will be like this, a great dimming in which all of their secrets will be very small things.

The newspaper is beside him. The surge has come after a debate, three days ago, when the candidate told the moderator—an anchorman from one of the large networks—precisely what he thought of the media and its polls. His campaign manager, a former senator herself, told him he had used the moment beautifully. He can speak this way, hotly and with great precision, on issues that he cares deeply about. He feels voters looking at him now with new consideration; *Perhaps it is possible,* they are thinking. *He has that timber, the looks, that presidential fire.* Crowds wait outside buildings, hands reach for him.

You go into heavily warm rooms where the flashbulbs fragment your vision into dark and light and someone is introducing you, saying, *The Senator from Kentucky, the next President of the United States!* The candidate concentrates on the breadth of his shoulders: he blinks his eyes with charm. He moves as a man at ease with the world, a man with crisp answers. Sometimes his speech is extemporaneous;

sometimes, when he is making a major policy statement, the words of a teleprompter hover to his left and right. He feels the campaign manager's fingers pulling him after, toward a reporter or to receive an honorary sweatshirt or cap; she keeps a smile—certain of his success—fixed in place. She is part of his conscience now, grounding him, bringing him always back to essential duties in these halls and rooms of light and possibility. He does not like to think of how her eyes cannot meet his when she hands him the hotel keys.

He turns the pages of the newspaper, just able to distinguish its contents in the failing light. A war rages in the Middle East. Outside of London, a ghost, a robed, hooded figure, is caught on closed circuit televisions at the palace of Henry VIII; the guards of the palace insist it is not a ruse. Nobody can explain it.

The doorway glows. The water falls. The prostitute has large, knowing eyes that turn to him in shadows. She will lie with him soon. This knowledge is wild, suddenly, in the candidate's chest. She will hold him down when she makes love to him, will tease and command him, and nearly always, when it is done, he weeps, and her fingers trace that wetness. She will move her body to him tightly, kiss his neck. They will talk and finally drift in and out of sleep. The phone will ring once.

Headlights from cars move over the wall. The candidate rises to close the curtains.

In Georgetown this afternoon his wife is giving a fundraiser. He imagines her standing by the stairway in a Chanel dress, wearing pearls, giving the caterer precise instructions. Their house is full of loud voices, and chandeliers are lit like bright ice. Tomorrow she will fly to be with him. She will hold him in front of crowds, moving into the embrace of his arm, waving with him, an act they slip into. But they have not made love for many years—not since the death, in infancy, of their second-born. The candidate thinks of his marriage as an old western, with all of these false fronts of saloons.

His daughter is in Vanderbilt, in Nashville, and soon will be home for the holidays. On easy summer nights, when she was a child, she walked with him, campaigning door to door. They handed out bumper stickers at supermarkets. He was the mayor of Glasgow then, running for state representative. There was the smell of tobacco farms, highways of dust. Oak trees grew wild against the red horizon. Every day, at four o'clock, thousands of blackbirds gathered in those branches. The candidate and his daughter watched the birds together. It was like a promise kept between them.

Honey, he tells his daughter, as he lies breathing in this hotel darkness, *it is not enough, the Western. But I'll do everything I can for you not to know this about me.*

For it could all unravel, if he does not control it: newscasters next to a bright graphic of his anguished features, telling a national audience about his fall from grace. His wife in video footage saying, *Yes of course I still love my husband but we have nothing more to say at this time.* Pictures of a hotel like this in New Hampshire, or Iowa, or South Carolina, reporters front and center with their microphones; shots of Vanderbilt, his daughter walking with her chin up, still believing in him, no matter what is shouted her way. Very much depends on him now, on keeping aware of each fragment: the candidate imagines a broken mirror of light and dark, all of these shards.

The shower has stopped. The candidate waits, hearing the sound of the shower curtain; his mouth is dry. The door is opening. The woman comes from the light.

YANK

ON the bus from Nashville to Lonoke, Arkansas, Jim Yankee Fish sits in back, in the star suite, with Bones, the bass player, while the star is up front doing business. The young and old singers all call Fish "Yank" when they see him in bars or on the road. *Yank,* they whisper, and he knows it, feels it like a hard strum of a guitar on his chest, came from Goddamned *Boston,* can you believe it? Had a couple of songs with other artists and one killer of his own; Fish feels it in the bright young eyes that look at him, saying, Give me your secret. Let me write one killer song, just to get me known. They want the secret to his beginning, but they do not want to know how to be what he is now, thirty-eight and obscure. They have their own plans for what they'll be doing when they hit thirty-eight.

Now he is on the road again, picking up a little change, a guest star of the Big John Casper show. Big John is a former *Hee Haw* star who has made his living since *his* star fell by renting out this and three other buses to major rock and country groups (the last, Fish understands, was the rock group Heart; "they're okay," Big John told him earlier, "no ripped upholstery") and living off some hits from his early days, and, like Fish, occasionally doing a television show. Last night Big John appeared on *Nashville Live,* and the band today is tired, sleeping in their bunks.

Fish's one monster hit was called "Say You're Mine," and was part of his hit album of the same name. The song became a country classic, though nobody else has recorded a chart-topping version since Fish's own, fifteen years ago. He wishes somebody had: he could use the royalties. He looks out the window at the morning and the rushing red clay walls of Route 40, making comparisons. Big John is a little older. He has the buses to rent, and a house in Hendersonville, where the stars live; he never was any songwriter, but he's got a good ear, and he's done some songs that others wrote (one by Fish) that he's managed to spin into hits. Fish had six months of brilliance, and then a wife who was a nurse with a drug problem. Since their divorce, he has had an apartment in Nashville which he helps pay for with maintenance work, and a cat named Elvis that he leaves with his landlord when he is gone.

Still, at times like this, with the wheels singing beneath him, Fish feels better about his life. It isn't every "star" who will let you ride in their suite, listen to their expensive sound system, and watch DVDs on their big screen. He likes being tight with Big John. He likes this brown and cream-colored vehicle: plush carpets, televisions, bunks throughout. It makes him *feel* like he was once, a star who belonged in a suite like this. And Fish has the respect that comes with being a has-been—the respect that comes from having *been there*—he sees that more often now in his chosen Tennessee home: this wishing in the eyes of young singer-songwriters who would die to have a hit on the charts, and a CD they could send home, to Iowa, or Kansas, or wherever it is they come in from for the American dream.

Bones lies on the bunk next to Fish, already sleeping with the seventy mph roll. Twenty-six years old and cowboy boots and jeans and jean shirt and woven Indian bracelets on his wrists. He's got some kind of nerve disease in the right arm that keeps crimping the right hand until one day, Bones has told him, the hand will not move. That doesn't seem to bother Bones like a night without drinking would, or a gig without a fat paycheck to go blow would. That is too far in the future. *I'll make my money by then*, Bones has said. *Who needs a hand then?* If Bones had his druthers, he'd play the Beatles and the Rolling Stones all day long. He has no medical insurance: he lives day to day, check to check. He chums around with Steely, the guitar player, the twenty year-old who ran away from home and who, for some reason, chose Bones as his mentor and friend. Fish has seen them, these youngsters who come into town, looking like gods and playing like the wind and setting no future up for themselves. Bones and Steely chuckle over women at the all-night stops, punch jukeboxes. They believe the future is infinite and full of money; they imagine pictures of themselves posed dramatically in music magazines, calls from all kinds of stars to do road work, publishers crazy about those songs they write on the road. They are polite, but they don't get too close to Fish.

Bones sleeps with his head heavily in a pillow, and Fish leans over to remove the glasses that are squeezing his nose. The bass guitarist moans at the metal sliding over his temples and turns his head away, toward the wall. Fish sets the glasses on the table, goes through the library of DVDs under the television. He chooses *Crocodile Dundee*, slides the disk into the slot, puts on headphones. The screen blinks at him: comes alive. It says *Paramount Pictures*. Fish rubs his eyes, shoves another pillow behind him on his bunk. He remembers the old, classic movies he liked to watch: the Columbia films that started out with a woman in a flowing gown on a pedestal, raising a torch to the sky as the music swelled around her, a glow behind her like a light from heaven.

"It's okay, baby," Marcia said to him in the dark. The Tennessee moon came through the window, making the tip of one breast, her shoulders, her face, a glowing white. "It's okay. You hold it like a dart and it won't hurt me any." She sat up and her hair fell over her shoulder and Fish wanted to kiss her, but she took the syringe from him and demonstrated how on his arm, not putting the needle in but touching his skin, a pin pressure, an indent. "It isn't good for you," Fish said. "Silly baby," Marcia said. "It'll be good for both of us." She put the syringe in his hand and lay back under that white moon and closed her eyes, and Fish went down to her thigh, holding the syringe like a dart, indenting, then puncturing, and Marcia made a slow sound, a pleased sound, an mmm, and he pushed the piston with his thumb until it was all in her, and he slid the needle from her and kissed the spot of blood, then moved a little and kissed the warm,

soap-smelling hair between her thighs, kissed her breathing smooth stomach. He darkened her breasts with his shadow and she reached down and held him while he grew hard and she watched his eyes. She said, "C'mon, baby," and soon he felt the Demerol working, making her loving frantic and long, and, deep in the night, when they had ceased lovemaking and she was sleeping, he curled close to the sensual curve of her back, and he could feel the feverish twitching of her muscles, a yearning: a dreaming of her soul long after her flesh was asleep.

Somewhere in front of the bus, Big John Casper is making his deals. He is a mountain of a man, dressed in a jean shirt and leather vest, a grizzled beard that he keeps barely trimmed, so that the bottom of his throat is still a pale, furry black. He has black eyes and laughs loudly: Fish hears him through the open suite door calling business partners on the bus phone and hamming it up with the driver. Big John Casper loves the wheel and deal, and that's the big difference between himself and Big John, Fish knows: Fish was never as bold in this business. Big John loves to call from his bus phone, loves moving about his home office in Hendersonville, the walls full of awards and CDs in frames and photographs of him keeping company with fame. He encourages the young ones, like Tellulah DuBois, the twenty-four-year-old knockout singer whose deep laughter Fish can hear up front now also, that sound a momentary stirring that makes him want to get up and go there and watch the way her chestnut hair moves, and her long, smooth legs that rise to pastel shorts. *Tellulah:* the name is smooth in his mind and he closes his eyes. Big John loves the young girls he can be a papa to; he loves sitting and typing the road schedules, the places they will go, the sizes of predicted audiences: *August 25: Lonoke, Arkansas, Dilly Regional High School, anticipated audience 500; August 26, 27: Shelbyville, Texas, Clear Creek Park Amphitheater, anticipated audience 2000. Autograph party afterward!* Big John keeps the wheels turning, his friends on the road, his CDs making money, the young girls happy and admiring. Big John with the white teeth. It is easy to love Big John. Big John, who met Fish for the first time, found out he hailed from Boston, and said, *Yank, what're you doing here?*

On the TV, the actress Linda Kozlowski fills her canteen at the edge of a waterhole, and Fish watches her along with Mick Dundee: her long legs, smooth back, cleft of spine. Fish has seen the movie a few times now, and this is his favorite part. With the exception of Tellulah DuBois, he has never seen a woman so beautiful.

"She's some looker," Bones says, awake now on the other bunk, his eyes blinking behind his glasses. He slips on his own headphones.

"Yes, *man,*" Fish says.

"I'd take two of her on a Popsicle stick," Bones says, loudly.

"*Amen,*" Fish says. He puts an arm over his forehead and watches until Crocodile walks through New York for the first time. The thing he likes about Mick Dundee is that he is an exile who knows how to make himself at home.

He sleeps through the rest of the movie. In that strange gray dreaming area he moves through a day a few weeks ago, mowing the lawn to earn his keep at the Nashville West apartments. He is sweating in the July sun. *Fish looks up to where the voice is calling him. "Hey," the woman says, and Fish can hardly see her with the sun high above. "Can you come on up here?"*

Fish goes up metal steps that resonate beneath his sneakers, and he thinks about this woman, whose name he does not know, who lies out often under the sun on the lawn he has just been mowing. She suns with her top undone and loose, so that with a little imagination Fish can feel his fingers brushing against the cloth strips over her chest and shoulders, the texture of that cloth: running the pad of his forefingers beneath the straps, then holding firm, pulling the top down. He would look at her eyes and there would be heat there, above the sexy pout of her mouth. He would kiss her dark skin and her nipples, and feel her body start to move with him.

She is pouting about the stove when Fish makes it to the coolness of her apartment, and he is suddenly aware of the hurt in his head from the sun, of the sweat running through the hair of his chest, down to where his shirt is tied around his waist. The woman's eyes notice, too. She has hair so black it looks nearly blue in the indoor light.

"You were some country singer once, somebody told me," she says, as the coolness moves through Fish like a new kind of breathing.

"I've done some," Fish says. He is glad that the arms of his shirt are hanging over his shorts. The woman is wearing a t-shirt, and she looks freshly-showered and clean, and Fish can see the outlines of the nipples he has dreamed about.

"Somebody also told me you were married," this woman says.

"I don't have her anymore," Fish says.

Fish knows this woman sees into his eyes, then: into a place where lately he wishes women could not see so easily. He lowers his gaze, and there is silence for a moment. He thinks about changing the subject back to the stove, but then thinks to hell with it. When he looks up again his expression has changed. He is not shy about anything now. Neither is she. "I guess you know where to find the shower in these places," the woman says, before she walks into the bedroom.

But the lovemaking is nothing like Fish has dreamed. The woman lies naked under cool sheets for him when he comes from the water, and he hardly dries himself, in his wanting of her flesh, liking the feeling of coming down against her with his wet skin on her smoothness, of going wild against her. But he also feels acutely his lack of knowledge about her—still, even, her name—a sensation that disturbs him for the first time in his life; their lovemaking is more athletic than passionate: more coolness than hot sun, too quick for sweat. Before he leaves, Fish promises to come back and fix the stove.

It is later in the day now and Fish sits with Big John in the high school theater, three hours before the show begins, watching the musicians and roadies set up instruments and amplifiers, connect cables. He can smell Big John's Old Spice cologne and feel his weight beside him; they sit with beater cowboy boots propped against the row of chairs in front of them. Bones is hitting some slap-notes; Steely tunes with harmonics; Jimmy Wiley sets up his pedal steel. Tom is trying the position of his bass drum, and Allen plays a few notes on the synthesizer. Then Tellulah walks in: Fish can see her coming from way back, where the black stage curtains are, through all the scattered boxes and wires and equipment, and through the band.

She touches Bones, Steely, and Allen as she passes them, and they straighten from their hunched positions and smile, and come alive like flowers under the sun. She walks up to the microphone stand in tight jeans that she has sewn patches of all colors on. She wears a white tank top that hugs twin curves of breasts, and Fish thinks about those breasts, chestnut hair, bare arms, green eyes, the fingers now lightly touching the stand.

"Sing a few, honey," Big John bellows. "Let's see how we sound."

The band kicks off, and Tellulah starts singing. Big John leans over to Fish and says, not for the first time, "Man, she's gonna *go* places." John says that about everybody he works with, but Fish thinks he might be right about this girl. She's already fronted some shows for Reba McEntire, and now she sings one of Reba's songs, her voice country-sad and full of wanting. She unclips the microphone and walks across the stage, and Fish knows that she's not doing a sound check anymore. He feels it as she does: she's singing to an audience that will be there tonight, and ten years from now. She's moving to the sound of Tom's click-track, to the rhythmic slide of Bones' bass, to the sad notes of pedal steel guitar and piano lifting and falling. Her hands reach to the imaginary audience as if reaching for a lover.

She goes through a few numbers, and then comes out to sit with Fish and John. She slides in next to Fish, touches his forearm. "Hi, Mr. Yank," she says.

"Sounds good, girl," Fish says, smiling.

"Mm *hmm*," Big John affirms.

'That's what I need to hear," Tellulah says. Her eyes and body, so close, flirt with Fish. He'd like to run his hand along those tight jeans, those tight legs beside him, to see what would happen. But it wouldn't feel right here, not with Big John, and he doesn't know exactly what Tellulah's flirtation means anyway. He's seen all kinds of flirtation in this business: performers wanting reassurance, women wanting a moment of love, and then forgetting you. Tellulah talks to John about the sound, and Fish watches her lips, her tongue wetting

their dryness, her eyes dancing occasionally with his own.

It is a place of gray Fish sees now. Not the brightness and precision of spotlights, nor the different hues in darkness with a woman he loves. It is a place of gray.

After the woman at the apartment complex, Fish went back to his place and showered again and sat on his bed with his guitar as evening fell, until he and the music seemed to blend with the shadows. He kept a beer by his side, and the darkness came completely and still he played, humming one melody over and over. It went from open C to F and made Fish think of a field in Massachusetts, of a bright day years ago: he could see trees bend and sway with gusts of wind, a hawk holding steady in the sky, cocking its head over the flowing grass. And then Fish realized, with that familiar rush, that the tune he was playing was new and it was his, and he switched on the light and, blinking, his spirit singing, he found paper and pen and a telephone book to write on and he went to work on his new song.

And then it is night and there aren't nearly the five hundred in the theater that Big John said there would be. Fish waits by a stack of crates at the side of the stage while Tellulah opens the show. She's dressed in a splendid white suit that is filled with sparkling gold and blue rhinestones. Fish can see, through the light of the stage, the shining eyes in the front rows of the audience, but there are dark gaps, too, of nothing, of vacant seats, and Big John comes up the back steps next to Fish and says, "Shee-it, Yank. I ain't pulling them in no more." Fish smiles and says, "Screw it, man. We're old farts anyway. But *she* isn't." They laugh and watch Tellulah, and Fish feels John go through his routine of mopping his forehead with a kerchief, sucking in his belly beneath a brown leather and rhinestone vest, and clicking his stage boots against the floorboards in time with Tellulah's last song. "Go get 'em," Fish says. "Come relieve me," Big John says, *"soon,"* as Tellulah is saying, "You saw him last night on *Nashville Live,"* and Big John's smile spreads for the act. He lumbers, mountain roly-poly, arms and legs shaking, clapping a cowboy hat atop his head, singing Chuck Berry's "Johnny B. Goode," out into the spotlights.

Fish goes down wooden steps, past fire hoses and ropes hanging on the walls, hearing Steely go into the ride. He goes to the men's dressing room, and the sound is more faint. There is a bench here, on the tile floor, under a light that flickers green, and clothes hanging from a portable rack. In the bathroom he urinates, then comes out and undresses, and puts on tight jeans, stage boots—lizard skin, the last gift Marcia gave him before she said she couldn't live his hours anymore and he said he couldn't live her habit anymore—and a white country shirt. He puts on a ten-gallon hat. He thinks about Chuck Berry singing in the stars: the article he read in some truck stop somewhere, about the capsule shooting through space with a drawing of a man and a woman, and a recording of Chuck Berry and the Beatles and Beethoven, *so that if another civilization finds the capsule,* the article read, *they will know what humankind looks and sounds like.* Fish walks out again, his boots echoing on cement, then on wooden steps up into the noise, to the shadows of stage right, and he is with the music, taking his guitar from the crate he leaned it against. It is a Guild F-50, the same kind of auditorium-body acoustic Elvis had once, too, when he was young and still a great singer and not yet a movie star. Fish throws the strap over his head and shoulder, plugs in his jack; he likes the reassuring feel of the roundback against his belly, the darkness he hums a few notes in, bringing the body of the guitar up to his ears, likes the bright slip of music and lights before him, too, the *smell* of music and lights: performers, crates, metal strings, wood, heat of drums. "All the way from Boston," a sweating Big John says now, above the driving beat, "one of the brightest lights on the Nashville skyline ... the Tennessee Yank him*self* ... Jim Yankee *FISH!!!*"

Fish hops across the stage with the rhythm, his upper body and guitar facing the audience, his eyes hard on his fingers. He hears yells and scattered, enthusiastic clapping; they recognize his song, and for a moment, even in the act, Fish could cry with the glad, huge feeling in his chest. The feeling sweeps his nose and eyes, and then he is back again, seeing his fingers hit A, seeing audience, seeing the windscreen of the microphone:

Well I'm so low-down, pushed-round, fightin'-mad
You're runnin' out on me with every fancy Dan
Before we're all through I'll ask you one more time—
Honey just for once won't you say you're mine

The audience is clapping, yelling, and to Fish's right a fat man is standing, pounding his fists rhythmically into the air beside a startled wife.

You are my heart-mate, soul-mate, one-time dream
Mississippi summer sunny dreamboat queen,
So baby save me a little bit of my pride—
Aw honey just for once won't you say you're mine

Fish looks back as Tom does the fill, sees Bones and Big John grinning. And he sees Tellulah, standing back at another microphone, watching him as she gets ready for the harmony, and watching him in another way, too, her eyes wet and full of hope.

Doncha think it's time you treat this old boy right?
Honey just for once won't you say you're mine

Steely goes into the ride. The audience roars. They like this one. It reminds them of a time they met a lover. It reminds them of a time with best friends in a bar. It reminds them of a summer night, a rustle of leaves. A high school prom. A mouth coming close to kiss. Fish tips back his hat, closes his eyes, hits E-sharp to A, feeling these chords through his fingers, his belly, his chest and blood and heart.

In between stardom and obscurity there is a gray place of thousands of dreams, Fish thinks, as he sings. You're a forever dreamer, Fish. But all you ever dreamed of was singing the songs for anyone who would listen: nothing else mattered. Others, like Big John over there, playing piano under the spotlight, thrive on the circus. Big John carries himself that way, loves the watching eyes, the applause and laughter, loves being a clown. I am somehow lucky, Fish thinks. I know the circus and also the great gray places, the great geography of dreams where songs are born.

***

It is midnight now in Lonoke, Arkansas. The band has showered and loaded equipment into the bottom compartment of the bus. Fish has breathed the hot, wet air of night, then climbed aboard for the short hop through the small town to the restaurant with the neon sign that reads *CATFISH ALL U CAN EAT.* Next to the sign is a giant blue bug-zapper. There are some cars and an old white ambulance in the parking lot, and Bones and Steely joke about the need for an ambulance in a joint like this. The inside of the restaurant is dirty: the tile floors have not been washed and the counter where they lean in to order is greasy. "It ain't the Ritz, but it's free," Big John jokes with his band quietly, leaning in to order steak, before going over to the table where businessmen of the town and their wives sit, back to his wheeler-dealer, happy-to-sign-autographs smile. Bones and Steely press a string of George Strait hits into the jukebox, and Fish sits next to Tellulah. He likes her clean smell next to him, like lilacs, her fingers resting lightly on the tablecloth. He watches the other diners, the regulars, their slumped backs at the counters, the teenagers, the workers getting off shift who sit at tables and look at the strange band of outsiders and do not talk. Tellulah watches Fish's curiosity, drapes her arm casually over the back of his chair, rubs his shoulder gently. He feels her hand like a moment of true, warm sun at the start of summer. They look at each other briefly and are sitting together that way when Bones, fumbling with his fork across the table, starts hissing, *"I can't feel the fucking fork I can't feel the fucking fork,"* his eyes wide and frightened, and then he is yelling and Big John is rising in the distance, through smoke and tables and diners, frowning, as if he knows already that this is going to be a serious situation and he'll have to take care of it.

"We'll fly a bassist down to Shelbyville," Big John says later, standing near Fish in the front of the cool bus, the lights out and illumination coming only from the driver's dashboard, so that Fish sees one side of Big John's face: an alert eye, a nose, black whiskers. Beyond Big John and the driver, Fish sees the endless dashes of highway rushing at them. He tells Big John good night and turns away, walks down the rolling runway, slides into a lower bunk at the side of the bus where he has stored his bags. He closes the curtain, and in that six-by-three closed blackness, he thinks about Bones, riding now in the star suite, speaking his fear to Steely in the darkness; Bones will fly back to Nashville for tests tomorrow, all expenses paid by Big John. And Fish will be—where had John said? Shelbyville, Texas. Fish remembers the copy: *August 26, 27: Shelbyville, Texas, Clear Creek Park Amphitheater, anticipated audience 2,000. Autograph party afterward!* Fish takes his digital player from a bag, cues up, hits play. He lays back and Reba sings softly to him in the night, slow and sad.

The curtain parts, and Fish feels rather than sees Tellulah sliding in beside him; feels her weight and female warmth nestle to him, smells her shampoo. He watches her face close to him: her eyes, nose, mouth, then feels her touch and settle against his neck. They do not speak. He holds her, feels her few years in her embrace. It makes him young, and Reba sings.

Fish is not sad; he doesn't know what he is, exactly. He feels like maybe he should go back with Bones. But Tellulah presses close, and he doesn't want to think about Bones anymore. He thinks about Reba's song, and the other music, too: Chuck Berry, and the Beatles, and Beethoven, that small, bright star singing to the heavens. He holds Tellulah tightly, and closes his eyes, and hums with Reba in the rolling darkness.

GRACEFUL LIES

All flesh is grass,
She says, naked
As the wind she stands in ...

And its loveliness
Is like flowers
Of the field on fire ...

DAVID DANIEL
God Appears at Night as a Burning Field

I

I USED to wonder what guys said about me in high school. It
wasn't the kind of wonder most girls have, an expectation: it was
more of a terror. I would go home after school and upstairs,
before I dressed to go out and play basketball with Julie and Teresa, I
would take off my clothes and go to the full-length mirror and look
at my body. I was very heavy then. *Penny Hyland,* the guys would
probably say—watching me in school hallways and on the bus—*big
tits, but* man—; then they would say the rest of it, about the rest of
me: the size of my thighs and belly. Girls whispered things, too, I
knew, their eyes running over me with pity, and often with disdain.
All of this gathered in my head as I watched my reflection, and I
would look away from the mirror as I put on my sweats.

This was in Goffstown, just west of Manchester, New Hampshire,
a long time ago. I didn't know much then, didn't care about anything
but eating and worrying about it and gossiping with Julie and Teresa.
When I was a junior I met Mike: he was a freshman, and a virgin, as I

73

was. The first time we made love there was not the pain I'd heard other girls talk about. We were at Mike's house and we did it in his bedroom while his parents were gone for an evening. I had a loose t-shirt on; I kissed Mike's ear, ran my hands over him to feel his naked-ness, loving it when he couldn't control himself anymore. He looked at my eyes afterward with wonder.

When Mike's folks were home I never felt any pressure, like I thought I would, being older. But then I realized that, even though I got on with Mr. Burnett, he thought of me differently than he talked to me. He was looking at me one evening from his brown wing chair in the living room, and we were talking about fishing, which we both liked. His eyes took me in politely, but I felt him thinking inside, *She won't lead my son somewhere he can't handle: heavy girls like this don't make love, do they?*

Mike and I probably looked awfully strange together. He was thin, and when we made love I stretched my hands across his shoulders and around his back. I was one hundred and ninety pounds then and gravitating between size eighteen and twenty dresses. We made love many times, and Mike used to say he loved me for something special inside of me, which when you got right down to it was the best I could hope for. But he liked physical things about me, too: he said I had a beautiful face, and beautiful lips and eyes.

I never tried to think I was thinner than I was or that maybe I didn't look so bad. I never lied to myself and I know many women do. That wasn't my problem. My problem was always in the knowledge of being overweight: that in presenting myself to others my weight was always there, in their polite eyes. The eyes are always the hardest thing.

After that night when I saw words in Mike's dad's eyes I started to work out. I'd taken diet pills before, but I'd never stuck to them: they made me sick to my stomach anyway. I'd convinced myself that working out would be the only way to get the weight down. So in the fall of my junior year, I started running with Julie and Teresa. That was a mistake because they were both thin and they ran in the mornings to keep that way and I tried to join in when they were at two miles a day. The first and second days they were patient with me when I bent over, after half a mile, tasting blood in my mouth and feeling pain in my thighs and wowing in my head. They said we could walk back, that really they'd had enough for the morning, and if they didn't get back soon and shower and put on their faces they'd miss the bus anyhow. Those were graceful lies that went on for two mornings and on the third morning out, when I bent over, and they stopped, I told them to go on. They did, reluctantly, and I watched their slender backs go over the small rise and curve off behind the pine trees. In that early morning light, my lungs still heaving, my hands on my hips, I walked home and watched things. The sun on the wetness of leaves and across the field at Shyer's farm seemed to set fire to everything: I have a feeling my condition had something to do with that also. I walked slowly and tilted my head back until I could smell things without a blood-smell, and walk without a headache.

Mike was nothing special-looking. He was quiet and had pimples, and like the idiot high-school girl I was, I eventually took him for granted, skipping some of our dates to go to the movies with Julie and Teresa. When he got angry I dropped him. He was stunned when I told him: we were in my old Chevy Cavalier driving back from school. He cried when we neared his house and that surprised me, because a voice inside me, the one saying, *Hyland, who really wants you the way you are?*— that voice suddenly had opposition. He told me to let him off there, before his house, so he could walk and not be in tears when he got home. I watched him go away from me, his sweatshirt rippling in spring wind, his head bowed, and I could not feel anything except *it would have happened sooner or later anyway*. But I grew to miss nights in town with him, at Goffstown Pizza, his grinning tomato-sauce teeth, and his dark, bright eyes.

I don't mean to make this all sound dejected, but you get that way.

You get that way when you are young and you want to be as slim and attractive as Teresa, with her long brown hair and her clear skin, and the guys look at her with desire in the lunch line and they look at you with something else. Some then look away with guilt, and others don't even have the tact to do that. They'll look at you, and back to Teresa, and you see in their eyes that they feel you are lucky to be with her. Teresa caught on to this, too, and in our senior year, she didn't sit with Julie and me at lunch anymore. She had lunch with the guys: we'd watch her slim waist and hips move flirtatiously every day as she came up to Jimmy Prescott's table, and her hands would go to his shoulders. She'd say a few words to Jimmy into his ear and talk to his friends and sit down with them. Julie and I often started our conversations at lunch by saying, *Look what she's turned into*, and by thinking, *Wish it was us.*

II

Julie was slim, but not what others called pretty. She sometimes had kind of an intense look when she stared at you, and her hair was cut square and short then. She would have looked better with a perm or a different style. She didn't see many guys either and so we spent a lot of nights out drinking when we were seniors: we would go to Mc-Donald's late and have coffee before we went home. Our parents trusted us; they rarely waited up. Maybe that's because they knew we weren't with guys, I don't know.

Once Julie and I drove to see the porn movies at a Drive-In over the Massachusetts line. We'd never seen those kind of films before, and I remember feeling weird, paying the lady at the booth you drove up to, then turning off the lights and slowing because I couldn't see and I didn't want to hit anybody. Julie was giggling that we were just *there* so she wasn't much help. First thing we see as we round the fence is this giant girl giving two giant guys blow-jobs, going from one to the other. The Drive-In was packed. There were cars at just about every slot and all of the speakers were taken, so we found a spot near the back and tuned in the static moaning on the radio. It surprised me that so many people were there. I guess I expected just dirty old men to go to those things, but during the intermission, where they flashed popcorn and Coke across the screen, plus some goodwill ads about pollution and played the national anthem, all kinds of people walked to the snack bar. Most of them were on dates: guys and girls, and they walked in clusters, laughing and talking. It was very funny for Julie and me, and we never told anybody we'd gone. But I thought for a long time about the women in those movies: not of their shame, but of the guts it took to be *seen* like that.

I was good at math especially, and I helped Julie get through a lot of high school exams. I never thought high school or any subject in high school would get me anywhere, but I won a couple of math awards as a senior and that helped me land a job keeping books at a company in Manchester called McGracken Resin. McGracken was in a run-down mill building on Canal Street, in one of the rougher parts of town, and I took an apartment within walking distance, over the river. My parents didn't like that I was living there, and we had arguments about it, but I wanted to be on my own. The people at the company interested me. Manchester is a small melting pot, a mini-New York City, and we had everybody working in the warehouse: French-Canadians, Puerto Ricans, blacks, Mexicans, Irish, Italians, you name it. Many were transients—just there a few months and gone. I got along because I treated everybody like human beings, which was more than a lot of those guys got from anyone. A few times I brought the warehouse men things I baked. I overheard Vince, an Italian guy, say once that he liked carrot bread. I was baking carrot bread that night and I thought it would be a nice thing so I brought him a loaf the next morning. I'll admit I thought Vince looked all right in jeans, too. He thanked me, and passed it around to his friends, and they said thanks, nodding and smiling. At lunch he came into the accounting office and his shirt and pants were smeared with dirt from loading resin barrels onto the trucks.

77

"So where are we going tonight?" he said. He was smiling, and I could see thin lines in-between his teeth. I'd never seen him show his teeth that much before, and it put me off a little, the way he hadn't taken care of them. He was probably thirty-five or so. His forearms had a lot of hair on them.

"Tonight?" I said.

"Where are we going? You know. *Out.* Have a good time."

I was flustered, the way he came on so direct like that. I told him I baked the carrot bread to be nice. He shrugged and smiled with those teeth showing, swaggering a little, keeping his eyes on me as he left the room. Melba Barlia, this smart Manchester girl who rarely expressed herself except with her dark, wide eyes, looked at me from over her computer, shaking her head and saying, "Don't be nice to them. To those guys. They all talk. That's stupid."

I worked later that evening than I should have. My thought was to give Vince and the others enough time to leave so I could walk out without them seeing me. So I changed into my sneakers and stepped down into the warehouse at quarter of six, seeing ahead of me puddles of water on the cement like dark, wavy mirrors. The lights had been shut down. I went between gray hulks of crates, barrels and fabric rolls, my footsteps echoing, *snick, snick,* like that. I was scared anyway, but I had a feeling that something more was wrong. Then there was a quick movement behind me, a hand across my mouth. I screamed, but he muffled it, pushing his hand hard against my lips and teeth. I breathed fast through dust and glue fingers. We echoed in there, as I tried to pull away. His other hand and arm squeezed into my stomach, and his body pressed to me, and he dragged me behind a large crate. I could hear our echoes through the warehouse, my throat sounds coming back high and pathetic, and his grunting. He pushed my head against the crate, keeping his hand over my mouth. I smelled wood, saw dark splinters. He pulled the other hand away from my stomach, pushed up my dress, ripped underwear: I felt the cut and tear of it at my flesh. Then Vince's hand moved across the small of my back, and lower, a feverish, sweaty-palm press. His rough cheek pushed against my ear, and his voice vibrated against my jaw. *"We're gonna fuck, Penny-girl. Don't fight me."* I heard his zipper and the elastic-snapping sound of his underwear being pulled down. I raised my heel and stamped backward, hard, putting everything I had into it. My heel scraped shin and landed on top of his ankle, and there was a *crack* and his scream of *"Fuck!"* echoing, ringing in my ear like an explosion, and his hands were gone and I turned back and Vince was writhing on the cement, howling that I'd broken his foot. *I hope so,* I thought. I kicked him once in the chest and then again toward the face, and he caught my foot with his hands and I stamped down and he howled again and let go, and I ran; I went straight for the door and did not look back.

Outside, cars were going by on Canal Street slowly, and traffic was jammed up on the Notre Dame Bridge. A neon Coca-Cola sign above was blinking in the early summer night. I ran by an old man who leaned against a building, flicking his cigarette onto the sidewalk. His eyes stayed with me carefully, following, and other men, coming out of a warehouse a block down, narrowed their eyes as I went by. I went up onto the bridge, stepping fast, my thighs feeling like they were trying to fail me. I walked hard for the opposite shore. Far below, through the steel grating, I could see the black Merrimack twisting and churning, looking like, just under the surface of the water there, something terrible was happening.

<u>III</u>

I quit the job the next day. I only told Melba why, in a phone call: how right she was, and to be careful. I wished in the weeks I'd worked there that I'd grown closer to her. I boxed up my few things at the apartment and moved home, telling my parents I might go to college, I wanted better things out of life than the resin company. They were just glad I was out of the city, though I could sense my mother guessing that more was wrong with me.

It was July then, and the crickets sang in the forest in the

79

evenings. For a while, I ate heavily, ignoring calories, the salad my mother tried, kindly, to push on me, and the many silences when my parents watched me and then each other at the dinner table.

"Jesus," my father would sometimes finally breathe, looking at me sideways. "Slow down a little at least, will you? You're gonna explode, eating that fast."

My mother would give him a hard look, and he'd shrug his shoulders and put his hands out and say, "What, damn it?" more loudly. He'd leave the table then and we'd hear the television switch on abruptly in the next room. My mother would raise her chin a little with her quiet dignity, and breathe carefully through her nose, and give me this thin little smile. I always acted like I didn't know what my father's problem was, but I could've dictated the conversations my parents had later on, behind my back:

Jesus Christ, Martha, the kid's gonna kill herself, eating like that.

I know, honey, but we have to go slowly. She's been through something lately. Maybe she'll tell us.

You always do this, Goddamnit, my father would say, making fists like he did when he was frustrated. *Forgiving every little Goddamned thing she does. Maybe she needs to face up to her problems rather than getting excuses from you all the time.*

You don't have to be so crude, Jim, my mother would say. I could imagine her jaw flexing the way it did when she got defiant. *You can't raise a girl by being so harsh with her.*

At night, on my knees in bed, when my parents were downstairs in front of the television shows, I pressed my forehead down to the mattress and cried, trying to trap it all in my throat, making sounds that I couldn't believe came from me, hearing an unreal pounding in my ears.

I took a job at Ford's Ice Cream in town. It was just down the street from the Little League fields, and Thursday and Friday nights, when I was put in charge, and after the Little Leaguers had come and gone, faces smeared with black raspberry and chocolate chip, I would clean counters until everyone had left. Then, grasping a cool ice-cream scoop, I made craters in the chocolate chocolate chunk, packing it into a plastic half-gallon container. I locked up and drove to Julie's, where she would give in to my teasing, coaxing voice, and we would eat on the front porch. I could tell sometimes that it made her sad, being a co-conspirator. We'd listen to the late-evening cicadas in the bushes on the other side of the road, doing what Julie called their Song of Love. When cars went by, I'd make up stories about the people in them and get Julie laughing. The ice cream was so good when it was a little melted, and Julie would close her eyes and *mmm* with the spoon in her mouth, and once and a while I'd see her face get serious, and I'd turn away before she could open her eyes to look at me.

Julie tried to convince me to go to the ocean with her, and I know that she wanted to encourage me, to show me that I was not the only heavy person in the world, to get me swimming in the sea, and I dreamed about it a lot and always refused.

"But you're so *beautiful,* Penny. I'm not bullshitting you. Your face is incredible."

"Don't start," I'd say.

"You don't see it," she'd say, quietly, "but I'm telling the truth."

My mother always said that, too, about my face, and the truth is I think I believed it in my bones. Mike had said it. But I took it a little more seriously when Julie said it. Still I only exposed the rest of me—of my body—when I was alone. On sweltering summer days I took long, lukewarm showers and dressed in cut-off jeans and a halter top, and then sat in a lawn chair in my back yard, feeling the shadows of trees move across my skin when the wind came.

In late August, during one of our chocolate chocolate chunk sessions, Julie invited me to join her Catholic young adult group for a weekend at their Marshall Lake retreat, twenty-five miles north in Jupiter. I went, really just for something to do. That's where I met Steve Gurczak. He was a bouncer in a Manchester club, and heavy himself, though not as bad as me: his belly hung over his belt and his shoulders and face were wide. We all gathered that first evening in a room made of stone. Candlelight flickered on the walls and made long shadows of eighteen of us. The group leader, a middle-aged woman with bright eyes and a low voice, talked about the world and how that was a fast place and this was God's place, and I could hear the waves of the lake down below on evening sand. I looked up and saw Steve watching me, his black curly hair unruly, his eyes fragile gray in the unsteady light. The next day we went together on our "trust walk." They blindfold you and a partner leads you on a path in the forest and you have to trust that he will lead you without letting you fall. Steve's hand was firm on mine, guiding me, and his voice was safe and interested in me. We talked about a lot of stuff and Steve got me laughing, telling me about some of the characters who frequented his club, a big place called The Phoenix—wild-looking DJs in their crazy costumes and cross-dressers and women made up so much that—as Steve said it—"they would be in real trouble in a rainstorm." He hated all the modern rock these days, he told me, the junk the DJs played; he liked live, pure blues. I said I did, too. We were way out on the path alone when thirty minutes into the walk Steve kissed me. I lifted up the blindfold and smiled at his big, handsome face, and put my arms around him. Beyond his shoulder there was a slope of pine trees and a needled floor and shadows, and the blue of the lake with golden flecks of sun.

Nights at Steve's apartment on Winter Hill, in an old brick building near the Bedford line, I watched our reflections in the black, glossy windows of his living room, and I liked what I saw there. It was good to make love again: Steve's hands pulling at me, his teeth finding my flesh, that moment when his body went beyond any thinking or control. Steve admitted one night that he liked watching sex films and was surprised when I said that I wanted to see them, too; in the living room, we piled TV pillows and blankets in front of his large television and put the tapes in the VCR: we turned out the lights and made love with that world of naked men and women in front of us, with their flesh-light washing over us, their whispers and moaning, and I felt like I'd been transported to some other land that I never wanted to leave.

In early winter I moved in with Steve and took a job at Eagle's Market, a grocery store in the General Stark Plaza, ten minutes away, as a cashier. My parents, being strict Catholics, weren't too keen on all of this, of course, but there wasn't much they could say about it, and I had a feeling that they were secretly a little relieved that I was gone. Steve worked the five to one shift at the club, and I would wake sometimes in the morning, while he was still sleeping, and pad my way through the warm apartment. At the kitchen window I looked over our small brick balcony, to steep, snow-glazed Winter Street; cars were frozen in a line there next to the sidewalks. A convenience store and some pink, clapboard houses glowed faintly at the bottom of the slope and, across Second Street, there was a cemetery where the wind made sculptures around gravestones, all of these crosses and monuments poking through the white. You saw trees behind them, before Route 293 and the Merrimack River: dark branches reaching into the pink sky. It was quiet there, and in early mornings, or in the evenings when I ate alone, I could hear the chimes our neighbors Roger and Carol had on the balcony below twinkling with sound.

I drove the old Chevy to Eagle's Market for my shifts. I'd ring lines of people up at the register and then sit in a back room and read and drink Diet Coke during my breaks—ten minutes off for every three hours on the job. One afternoon, leafing through a magazine I'd taken from our display rack, I came upon a full-page ad; it was for body lotion, promising to make your skin tighter and more glowing. The model was completely naked. She stood, holding a towel to her chest, investigating her backside in the mirror. Of course she had a wonderful, graceful body. Then I looked closely at her face: full lips, wide green eyes, a slight cleft chin—*my* face, nearly. And something

Julie had said came back to me as I sat there, my chest and arms and legs feeling like they were floating in that bright room. *Your face is so incredible, Penny. You'd be devastating if you got slim.* Julie was right: I could look a lot like this woman. The caption of the ad, rising above the product name, said, *One glance in the mirror says it all.* Nothing, all my life, had been more true.

I could hear my heart in my ears. I bought the magazine before I left that day, and cut out the ad and made two copies and taped them to our refrigerator door and bathroom mirror. Even Steve said it was amazing, how much I looked like the woman in the picture.

I started to diet, then. I was serious about losing the weight this time, and didn't care if I died doing it. I ate salads at first, cautiously, and stocked up on chicken, fish and raw vegetables, relying on articles from the women's magazines. I spent time learning how to prepare low-fat meals. On weekends I stopped at bookstores, running through titles like *The Junk Food Withdrawl Manual* and *Women's Guide to Weight Loss and Better Health.* For breakfast, I still scrambled three eggs for Steve, but boiled one for me, and sometimes had yogurt and strawberries also. Instead of driving to work, I'd walk the chilly mornings and afternoons to and from my job, feeling every day a little thinner, healthier, my woolen shawl warm around my neck and cheeks, my face flushed.

After a few weeks of the walking I started to jog home, changing in a back room and listening to the encouragement of the other women smiling from their registers as I passed them in my ski jacket and sweats, a rucksack on my back. It was a tough run that I could hardly make at first without slowing to a near-walk as I neared Winter Hill, my sneakers pounding on the sidewalk, past houses with crests of snow on the porch rails, past lights going on inside in late afternoon. And me, pounding and feeling fat and sick by the graveyard, this blood-taste deep in my lungs and in my mouth. The pine branches over the graves were bowed with ice, and dirty snow was laced around the stones, and I crossed the street and started up the hill, past Lac's Market, keeping the image of the model—I called her my Thin Twin—in front of me as I pushed on. I'd pick up my head and keep going at it, one foot in front of the other, and finally I'd make it to the apartment parking lot and turn and stand, heaving, on the porch, leaning on the mailboxes, the nausea coming in waves until my breathing had slowed enough that I could go into warm air, to stairs and shower.

Soon the hill became a little easier, and after a month of running back to the apartment I started running in the other direction as well, to the Bedford Gym, and swimming, then lifting in the weight room. Three days a week I did squats, leg-lifts, bench presses and sit-ups, feeling sweat come over my eyebrows and the wonderful soreness of my stomach muscles that told me I was losing, getting stronger. Pounding headaches came at me in waves, with moments of exhaustion and hunger that made me want to quit, rest a while, drive to the pizza joints and eat until I couldn't anymore. But I would finish my routines and go into the shower, watching other naked women through steam and spray, their trim bodies turning. I dressed and walked home past McDonald's and sub places and Papa Gino's with a new determination, home to salads and soups, to dry toast and ice water.

I met Carol outside by the dumpster in early March. It was bright and warm, and the tar of the driveway was wet. She was struggling to get a large bag of garbage over the metal-sheet side, and her scarf was waving about her head.

"Here, Carol, let me help."

"Oh *hi*, Penny. Thanks." And then: "*Jesus*, you're *lo*sing."

The pride in her voice sounded familiar, and I realized that I was thinking differently about myself. It was a new feeling.

IV

Some nights, when Steve came home, I would be on the living room floor, naked and with just a blanket covering me, on the pile of pillows that we left there always, and there would be a sex tape in the VCR that I'd paused, momentarily, when I'd heard his car in the lot below. The film-lovers would tremble there, halted in mid-ecstasy, and I would watch Steve step in, the shape of him, knowing that he was seeing less of me than he had four months ago. I could feel him smile, and he would say, "You're looking fine, Penny. Real good." He would grin at the TV and go shower and come back and lay with me and we would make love listening to the moaning, the startled gasps, of the actors, their light-motion over us. I'd wrap my legs around Steve's back and thighs, and he would finally shudder against me, his chest quivering against my breasts, and put his face into the curve of my neck and I would feel him relax and move into sleep and I'd click the remote off and we would lay there in the darkness sometimes into morning.

There were other times when he came home very late, silently, needing me awake. I would sit up in bed and say, "All right, hon?" He'd walk around and not say much and then lay with me: dark curly hair beneath my chin, my fingers working through it. There had been fights outside the club those nights—there was a lot of this starting to go on in the city, kids coming up from Massachusetts, gangs fighting over drug territory. Once he could not talk for a long time, because he'd been the one who found a seventeen year-old, in the Phoenix parking lot, shot in the face. That night, he put his head on my stomach and made sounds in his throat like he was trying to talk and then he cried and said, "These fuckin' Ricans," over and over, while I held him and rocked him in the darkness.

By late that summer I was down to one hundred and twenty-six pounds. On weekends, when Steve and I could have lunch together, and I was cooking, I could feel his body in the doorway behind me, watching. He would come up and slide his arms around me and put his hands on my still very large breasts and say, into my hair and ear, "Holy shit. Nice, Penny." I would turn and poke him playfully in the stomach and say, "Now we have to work on *you*."

Julie, from summer school in Vermont, wrote me letters of encouragement when I sent her reports on the falling numbers of my scale. Her postcards arrived with smiley faces, saying, *I'm so proud of you, girl!* My parents were glad, too. One hot summer evening, as I got out of the car on a visit home, my mother held out her arms to hug me, her eyes wet: behind her, in the doorway, my father smiled and cleared his throat and looked down and rattled the ice a little in his whiskey glass.

People in church noticed me, also; at Mass, at Our Lady of Montserrat in the city, dressed in a new, conservative skirt and blouse, I could feel eyes on me, approving, and that vast angled space was full of echoes; I sensed a connection with all the voices, saying in response to the priest *and also with you.* Afterward, walking out, the priest smiled and jousted with Steve; other people who, along with Steve, had been long-time members of the congregation, greeted us enthusiastically. Steve held a hand at the small of my back, and men punched him lightly in the shoulder. Women took me in with bright smiles and asked me which church I'd been with before, and said that Goffstown was a lovely little place, just the kind of quiet village they hoped they would settle in after a few more years in Manchester.

The heat got so intense that August that when you walked downtown you could see dark lines swimming on the tar up ahead. The sky over the old mill buildings was this hazy blue and it seemed like there was too much brightness everywhere, too much dust, too much traffic. But everywhere, in that heat, or inside, in dimness and sudden air-conditioning, I could feel men's eyes: on my breasts, my hips, my legs. They watched quietly and did not seem to understand that I knew exactly what they were doing: it was almost as if *I* wasn't there—just my body. I loved it. At the bank or the post office, the female tellers and cashiers, when I got up to them, would look at my eyes, my skin, my lips.

Steve and I had a picnic one Saturday that month with Roger and Carol at the sea in Hampton. I couldn't believe how beautiful the stretch of blue ocean, the white surf was. The sand stung my feet when Carol and I ran to the water. Roger and Steve sat under umbrellas, on towels, and drank Millers. The two of us girls shouted and teased them about bravery, then dove in. I felt the shock of cold, the water pulling around me, and came up laughing, my black one-piece wet and clinging. The ground seemed to slip away underneath me, making me fall into sand and foam. Gulls sailed in the wind just above us, eyes looking sharply down. When we stepped back up onto the beach, I could feel Roger's eyes on my hips and body, and I moved for him as I walked. Then I saw Steve's eyes on Roger. I walked and felt the sun on my skin, and Carol breathing by my side.

I didn't see things changing with Steve at first. He started going out and drinking a lot with some of the other Phoenix guys after work, and he would call at midnight and tell me *Don't worry, babe, I'm with Pete and Ralph and we're having a couple.* I would tell him to make sure whoever was driving was sober, that I could come drive if they needed. I knew the club had been a pretty terrible place with the fights lately, so I didn't object much. In the background I could hear the laughter of men and women, and music, and I imagined Steve pressing a short finger to his ear, breathing out carefully to mask his impatience, his eyes closed, trying to concentrate on my voice but wanting to get back to his friends. I would put on a false brightness, and tell him to relax, I'd see him when he got home. *I won't be long, Penny,* he'd say, blowing out his breath. *I just need to do this for a while, okay?* I'd say I never said he didn't, and we would sort of make up for the weirdness, but not completely.

But the drinking and going-out became constant and I started wondering who else Steve was seeing. He stopped calling me from where he was, and when I asked him about it he'd say, *It's ridiculous, I feel like I'm calling my mother. None of the other guys do this shit. It's just me running over to the phone to make my report.* Actually, I told him, I never asked for him to call—I'd just gotten used to him doing it. *Whatever, Penny,* he said. Soon he would not talk when he got home, at three or four in the morning. I would be awake in bed, smelling the clean pillowcase, listening to the late summer noises of the city: cars hushing by on Second Street and the soft blow of a freight train going south and crickets in the weeds at the back of our building. I'd hear Steve's tires crackle on pebbles and tar, and the engine being cut: silence again, crickets. I'd put my head deep in the pillow and listen to his unsteady steps on the last stairs, his key in the door. I would turn to the wall as he came in, listening to him, imagining him watch me, how the sheets rose and fell, if my breathing was slow and deep enough for sleep. He'd undo his belt, then the zipper, and I would hear the rustle of his shirt and wonder who he'd been with that night and maybe some nights I was wrong.

"Who were you with?" I'd say.

"I thought you were asleep."

I would turn back over. His silhouette was there, against the lamp in the hallway. "Who were you *with.*"

"The guys. With Pete and Ralph. We took it back to Pete's place after having a few."

"I called Pete's wife. She didn't know where you were."

"That must've been before we got there."

"Yeah, that must be it."

"Get off it, Penny."

"Where were you?"

"I said get *off* it."

I watched him: his big, dark shape. There was always a smell of liquor and cigarette smoke in the small air between us. I imagined Steve and his friends at the strip joint out on Route 101, rolling in there buzzed, laughing, taking in the new bodies: women dancing beneath the stage lights. I'd turn back to the wall and clutch the pillow and hear Steve go to the fridge, heavy footsteps in the kitchen, the whir of the refrigerator as he opened the door for beer. Then the TV came on, male and female voices with that TV energy, violins in the tense parts, the voices sometimes rising so that you could understand them, then dropping again.

In my nights alone now, I watched the tanned, soft skin of the sex-film women, their eyelids falling with pleasure, their mouths opening as if they might never take in enough air. I closed my eyes and listened to their soft, urgent voices. After a while I switched off the tapes and went into the bathroom; I'd slip off my nightshirt and turn in the mirror and look at myself. I used my Thin Twin's cream, always right there by me on the counter, smoothing it over the stretch marks at the lower part of my stomach, angling down; there were lines on my thighs too and at the top and sides of my breasts, but none of these were too bad. I rubbed the cream into my skin and turned in the mirror. I combed my hair and watched my face and moved my lips and eyes like the pornographic women did: without fear, and always in invitation. Sleep would hit me at about two, and I would go to bed, into dreams of skin: breathing, stretching, touched by fingers, by tongues and lips.

In the mornings Steve was there, on the living room couch, his head back, mouth open, beer on the floor, the screen quietly busy with the black and white *F-Troop* or *The Lone Ranger*. I'd make scrambled eggs and bacon, hoping these smells would wake him. Finally I would shake his shoulder, say, "I have breakfast, Steve, you hungry?"

"No, no," he would say, getting up.

"I'll be going to work," I'd say, and he would be heading for the bedroom, the main bathroom, his back to me. I'd say, *"Steve,* what did I *do?"*

"Don't *start,* Penny," he'd say. "You didn't do anything. Just forget it."

"You're so fucking *mad,* all the *time,* Steve."

"I'm not mad. Go to work."

There would be the sound of the shower starting, perhaps something tumbling off a shelf in there, Steve saying, *Fuck.* I would sit at the kitchen table for a second, trying to figure out if I should push him for answers. Then I would take my rucksack and go out the door, shutting it behind me quietly, and down the stairs.

V

Late on a September Tuesday night I drove to the Blues Union club, up on Elm Street. There was a good crowd there, pressing into the entrance, and the music of a rhythm and blues band pumping through; I squeezed through the people and the music seemed incredibly, frighteningly loud at first. I found a clearing.

I had dressed in a long black knit dress with a tank top, and black sandals; I wore three golden bracelets on my right wrist to set off my skin and eyes. I'd shaved carefully and taken a long time to prepare. I ordered a toasted almond, and stood in the corner where it was darker. My hand on the cool glass felt weak, as if at any moment my fingers might let the drink slide and shatter to the floor. I drank and watched the band playing. The harmonica player was amazing, the other guys in the band smiling and nodding when he went into a solo. I felt men around me staring and two came over and asked me to dance and I shook my head no thanks, not yet. After three drinks I could feel the bass notes in my stomach. The music went right through my legs, into the bones of my feet, up into my jaw. Now the bass player, dark-skinned, black and maybe Puerto Rican, was at the microphone, singing *Blues With A Feeling*, and there was a group of women dancing in front of him, their arms in the air.

From the dance floor, men and women turned to look at me, their faces all shiny with the lights and the drinks. One woman, close to me, had sweat in the hollow where her throat met collarbone. She held her man's thick shoulder, her fingers spread, long and white; she studied me and gently pulled him closer.

There were a lot of men in there, mechanics, businessmen in loosened ties, workers from the shops and factories, some guys from the city colleges. Some of the businessmen had gotten off the bus from Boston and, like Steve, were not going home. Others had hit

91

bars before this one and their voices were loud and happy.

A man in front of me looked nice. His hair was short in the back: black, bristled; he had this strong neck and shoulders. He wore a blue cotton shirt, the sleeves rolled up over the elbows. He didn't know who I was. He didn't know anything about me. He was tall and had a straight back and when he leaned down to listen to a friend shout above the music, I could see that he was not smoking. That was good. I didn't want to be tasting smoke. I watched him drink two whiskeys and hoped he wouldn't leave. He didn't. On his third drink I walked up behind him and ran a hand lightly across his back, then down his spine, and he turned. I said, "Wanna dance?" and even though he couldn't hear me he understood and I smiled at his surprised eyes. I liked his tanned face and even teeth. On the dance floor I held him close, with my head at his chest and my hands stroking his neck.

I followed him to his place on Massabesic Street. It was in an old, wooden apartment building, and our footsteps on the dirty stairway sounded like sandpaper. I was pulling at his clothes before he locked his door. He turned and grinned down at me, pretty drunk, and brought me into his bedroom. We left the lights off, and he finished stripping the clothes that I had started on, and took off mine.

Driving home three hours later I cried some; above me, sleeping birds on telephone wires were like black stars strung on a line. The wet sidewalks of Second Street, the Esso and Hess stations and the car wash and the banks and bars and restaurants, dark now, seemed part of some world I'd left behind and could never return to. A barn hawk, high above, glided in circles over Winter Hill: you could just see him against the clouds. The graveyard was a jumble of dark, rounded shadows, and a breeze moved through the cemetery poplars and pines. Lac's Market was opening, a bright wedge of light through the morning darkness. When I walked into the apartment, Steve was in front of the TV; the sound was off, and there were bottles on the floor around him, but he woke up as I came in, as I was taking off my sandals.

"Where were you?" he said.

"Out," I said, going by him to the bedroom.

He got up and caught me by an arm. "Out *where.*"

"Let go of my arm."

He did. He said, "Great, Penny. So you're getting me back. Just don't bring your diseases here. There's enough diseases in your head."

"I was fucking somebody. And he was *good.*"

I saw his quick, angry eyes, his hand coming from the side, felt the solid contact with my jaw, heard this thin note in my head. I fell against a lamp table, onto the floor. I saw my shoes fall and clatter, dust-balls on the floorboards, my hands shaking there. Steve kicked the lamp table and I heard the lamp break beside me. I rolled over, got up, and started for the kitchen, not looking back.

"*Pen*ny. Get back here, God fucking damn it—"

I pulled a drawer open near the sink. There was heat in my head, my jaw: my hand grasped the handle of the boning knife. Steve was in the doorway, and I turned to face him. His fingers were tight and thick on the molding: he stared at me, at first furious, and then, seeing the knife, in disbelief. I straightened my arms and held the knife forward in both hands, feeling like my body was rising three feet above me.

"Go ahead," I said. "Try and hit me again. I don't give a *fuck* about *anything* anymore."

"Penny," his voice dropped, and suddenly his face trembled all over. "I didn't want to hit you—"

"Get out."

"Jesus, c'mon, Penny—" his eyes filled, and he wiped a hand angrily across them.

"Get *out,* Steve. I fucking mean it. Now."

His shoulders went down, and his face just suddenly looked tired. He wiped wetness from his cheekbones. He went into the living room where I could not see him while I stood there, the knife in front of me, and I stayed like that until he went by me again, his head down, and out the front door. I heard the door click shut and his footsteps and then his car starting, rolling, driving away.

I lowered the knife and went into the bedroom. The suitcase was in the back of the closet and I dug it out, threw it on the bed, and placed the knife next to it. Carol knocked on the front door once, inquiring, afraid, and I called out that everything was okay, sorry about the noise, and I heard her footsteps go tentatively down the stairs again. While I packed, my eyes kept moving to the knife to make sure it was still there, and I listened for the return of Steve's car in the driveway. It did not return, and I knew that I would never again listen to that sound. I went through closets and drawers: panties, bras, blouses, skirts; my nervous fingers ran up dresses quickly, grabbed and threw sizes twenty, eighteen to the floor. I packed new dresses, the ones that fit me. The others could stay with Steve.

I took the pictures of my Thin Twin from the refrigerator and the bathroom mirror, folded them carefully, put them in my purse. I went down dark stairs, outside to cement steps and pale morning light. Everything was moist: leaves, dumpster, street, buildings. I held the suitcase tightly and walked fast to the Chevy, thinking of the knife on the bed, the room, clothes, all wildly frozen now in the light of our bedroom window. Far off, I could hear city sounds, but here the air was quiet, like the strange, still air you breathe before a summer storm.

LUNA

THERE are the towering trees, dark, like judges in their robes. These are in your dream, your memory. There is the traitor, begging. You wake with sweat on your cheeks and throat. Your wife rises with you into a night so humid it is as if you are entering water.

You are eighty-five now (can this be?—walking down the dark hallway you might be a ghost without flesh, but your knees, your hip, these remind you that you are, still, physically in the world). Your wife is seventy-one. The two of you move from the dream (the quick turn of your head, the intake of your breath that woke her) into night shadows; the hallway opens to pale field out the kitchen windows, the white smudge of barn. You imagine a silver flank of one of your horses, a muscular shifting, the smell of hay.

Your wife says: "Shall I turn on lights?"

"Nay," you say. "Leave it."

This darkness is easier. Not the darkness of memory, but of southern New Hampshire, the Merrimack River just beyond the hills, your old age in America.

"I'll fix coffee, drahoušku," she says.

Hovering outside the sliding screen door is your wife's garden, roses a white cloud close to earth. The moon is steady above the great mountain there, high in the vibrant stillness.

In your sleep, in your history, it was a summer night in the heart of Nazi-occupied Europe. You were twenty-four, dragging the traitor out of his stone farmhouse—a fat, middle-aged man, a village accountant; he was sweating and begging, his wife clinging to your arm. She said, *Nay nay nay,* weeping. You hadn't expected that—that a woman could love such a man so. You shook her off. The accountant—Sladec—had a daughter and son fled to England, the son fighting with the British forces. How could the man have been a traitor, with that son fighting for the Allies! He had seemed so committed to the cause! But Sladec had given many, many names to the Gestapo.

You heard the horses in Sladec's barn shifting to the commotion of your taking him: bucking, anxious. The moon was high, staring over the dark hills. The wife had dropped and was on her knees in her nightshirt behind you. It was a Goddamn mess, a horrible thing. She was saying, *Jesus and Mary I knew this, I knew it would happen.* Slapping her arms at the earth. There was nothing she could do—the phone lines were cut and the farmhouse was three miles from Kladno: you left her there with two of your men and pushed her husband on and fixed your heart like a stone.

The charges against the traitor were read in the forest nearby, with the towering trees all around. The moonlight broke through the branches, fell in fragments on the forest floor. Eight members of the Resistance cell surrounded Sladec, testifying, their shadows in motion; *Mr. Sladec betrayed Mikoláš and Petra and Velna, ages twenty-three and twenty-six and seventeen: they were beheaded and their heads displayed on spikes before the house at number twelve Lusace Seminary Street, Prague. Tomáš and Aleš and Jakub and Antonín were captured on June 14, 1943: after torture they were shot by a firing squad ... only Mr. Sladec could have compromised them ...* The traitor's face, hemmed in by evidence of his own treachery, was an astonished oval. Crickets were singing. There was the smell of sultry black summer.

In the Gestapo cellar on Vinohradská, in Prague, men and women you had recruited and trained had been drugged and beaten and slowly killed because of this man. Some before death were shown the heads of loved ones in fishbowls. You forced yourself to think of this. Of brave patriots suffering horribly, their last visions those of

the Gestapo: Gestapo fists, hard Nazi faces, the harsh voices echoing. Ugly, white-tiled walls with meat hooks near the ceilings, bright
acute light. Blood in the table scuppers. There was a guillotine in the
center room of the Gestapo basement that had finally killed many of
your fighters. All because of this lying, turncoat son of a bitch.

He bolted toward the darkness as he was pronounced guilty. It
was your job as the leader to stop him; you ran, you grasped the back
of his collar tightly in your fist. He fell to his knees, pleading, and you
put the 7.65 Mauser to his head and fired, feeling the concussion, the
weight of that head through the exploding metal, the sudden, no-
more breathing stillness of the body.

You lowered the man: here was the broken flesh and skull. The
others stood about you in a circle, knowing that it was the only thing
that could have been done, that more patriots would have died if
Sladec were left alive. *Even if you locked him up somewhere, even if you
hadn't administered justice, who would have watched him for the whole damned
war? No, it was the only thing.* A wind came through the forest, shifting
trees. The moonlight flickered on the ground. You imagined the wife
hearing the gunshot, the single, echoing report.

***

There is the smell of coffee now, the heat of it coming to your fingers. The lights are still off and there is the field, the white cloud
close, sailing at the earth.

Your wife watches your face. She puts down her coffee and takes
you by the hand. She slides open the door and leads you out to her
garden. You have trouble with your knees and hip, a little trouble
with your balance. You cannot see much. The darkness is all around,
sultry like that Bohemian night when you were twenty-four, when
you were as strong as all the world. The crickets are singing and there
is the astonished moon over the mountain.

There are smells of thyme, artemisia, sage. Your wife is talking
about the white roses, saying things, speaking Czech to you. She dips

a hand into the cloud, brings a stem, a white explosion forward. "Here, drahoušku," she says. "You see now? Here."

The moon is relentless: it is everywhere, it is even in the eyes of your wife. But you concentrate on her voice. You feel her touching your cheek, rubbing your back; in this night thick with water, she guides you, and you lean down and smell the rose.

LIGHT WINGS

With love's light wings did I o'erperch these walls,
For stony limits cannot hold love out,
And what love can do, that dares love attempt.
Therefore thy kinsmen are no stop to me.

WILLIAM SHAKESPEARE
Romeo and Juliet

THE play has not started. The crowd is still coming in, women and men in close-fitting overcoats, bringing with them the winter cold, the wind and rain of the Atlantic sea. They come from restaurants, a pleasant sound still in their voices, delight at their dash through the weather. Some are shadows moving over the glowing red curtain. A small orchestra below tunes up: a viola mourns; a bassoon goes up the scale. A percussionist hits claves, tabor, a bass drum.

The man sits with the woman. They are new lovers, and the man feels he is still in the sea of her, in the hotel bed, her smooth limbs like waves. The whole continent is falling into winter darkness. Cars are rushing over dark highways, swooping under bridges and building windows. The lovers lean close, in this theater; when the woman turns to the man, her eyes are bright crescents, her hair deep black. Her voice is low. He watches her lips.

He saw her for the first time on a cobblestoned street in another seaport, eight days ago, a few towns south. She was looking at scarves and skirts in a window. He came up and said, "You probably won't believe I'm interested in skirts," feeling his heart beat in his throat.

"If I did," she said, smiling, "I don't think I'd be interested in

99

what you're offering."

She was open, her smile immediate and honest. She wore a dark coat, a bright, green-print scarf that matched her eyes. Somewhere, distantly, the man felt his wife's scorn—she would mock him for this foray into youth. She would tell him that, as always, he was dreaming. But the woman at the window had a stunning, inviting face, and no scorn for him. They talked for a few moments there at the store window.

There was a fog over the town. Christmas lights were atop the shop entrances, making halos in the mist. A carriage, drawn by clopping horses, went by on the street beside them. You couldn't see the ocean, but you knew it was there, very close.

It was as if the man and woman were at the edge of the world. They walked together. She was from Wisconsin, she told him. Her husband was of old Madison wealth, and in and out of rehabilitation facilities with his alcoholism. In a marina a few blocks down, stays tapped against masts, a lonely winter sound.

"I live on Lake Michigan," she said. "I would have liked to live on the sea. Do you live here?"

"On the South Shore," he said. "I'm supposed to be on business, but I've probably been fired by now. I've just been driving."

He could feel his confession move her, and when he looked up, her eyes were narrowed with consideration. Another carriage went by them: the driver in a top hat, a few passengers, men and women speaking easily, fading in the fog.

The man and woman ducked into a coffee shop. A gull cried somewhere in the raw day. Bells rang out cheerfully over the door. They took a table near a window.

"So you're driving?" she said.

"I spend all day in a glass tower," he said. "And I come home in the darkness."

"What do you do?"

"Financial analysis. For a firm downtown." *But not anymore.* It had been four days now. The firm would have called his wife. She was in

South Carolina, but she would have surely contacted a neighbor to check on the house. His cell phone was on the kitchen counter, with his note:

Dear Margaret: There is no reason to worry about me. I am fine, and I know when you get over your anger you'll see my leaving was best for both of us.

His wife could call the firm, since she had insisted he keep working there; she could tell them anything she wanted, make herself a fucking martyr. He didn't care. She would be furious; she would be on the phone with her mother and all of her town friends; he imagined her at the resort, a cell phone at her ear, gesturing with her hands, raging, planning. The sea outside coming onto the cold shore, thin and hissing.

In the café a waitress came then for their order. There was a small crowd, people laughing and talking in conspiratorial tones, the sounds of dishes, a coffee machine, fork tines, knives on plates.

Soon their hot chocolates came, with bowls of steaming minestrone soup, crackers, bread. A car went by the window, rumbling over stones; it turned up a side street into the fog. For a moment you could see a church spire over the town, and then it, too, disappeared.

"My husband started his cycle years ago," the woman said. "Everybody covers up for him at parties, and he just gets blitzed and soon he's drinking all the time again and back in the hospital— sometimes we just say he is on business in Jakarta, because his family has offices there, but it doesn't fool anyone. Are you married?"

He'd taken off his ring the day he'd started driving. It was strange how easy it had been: just slipped it into the plastic cave of the glove compartment, closed the small door with a competent *snap*.

A great beauty simmered in his new companion; her eyes were wide and pretty. She was perhaps in her late twenties or early thirties. Worry, over time, had pressed something grave into her face, thin lines into her forehead. There was the sweep of black hair that she traced back with her fingertips. A triangle of winter light fell on her cheekbone when she talked, when she turned toward the window. People went by out there, ghosts walking. She watched them; her lips were a dark shade of red.

It was the first time the man had thought, truly, of cheating with anyone.

"My wife wouldn't care much," he said.

"About?"

"Being here with you."

"Where is she?"

"Hilton Head," he said, "vacationing. I made the mistake of not taking a job with her father's bank when we married four years ago, and she hasn't forgiven me. So she takes daddy's money and goes south, even now, at the age of thirty-nine—"

"You should be respected for being your own man."

The man shook his head *no*. "I've been married twice to wealthy women who wanted me to be more ambitious financially. Emotionally, it's like she's on the moon. I just don't seem to learn that things will end up this way."

"You have kids?" she said.

"No," he said. "You?"

"Yes," she said. "A girl. She's eight. My heart and soul. She's with her grandparents in California for a couple of weeks. I'm supposed to be with friends here."

He imagined her alone in the huge house on Lake Michigan, lion-tipped balustrades and a twisted winter garden and the flat, violet horizon. Waiting for her daughter to come home from school. The phone ringing, distantly, in hallways. Sometimes she answered, "No, I'm sorry. He's on business in Jakarta. Can I tell him who called?"

***

They are making love in every North Shore hotel or bed-and-breakfast that catches their interest. They turn his SUV into a new one every night, progressing up the coast. Soon they will be in New Hampshire, then Maine; when they speak of going all the way to Nova Scotia, the man thinks of a television advertisement: a windjammer cuts across ice blue of ocean, whales rise to the ocean's surface in great curves—relentless, singing, breathing life.

Each moment of flesh is a precious release. The man stares at the sweat of his lover's neck, the light of her eyes. He kisses the curve at the deep of her back, turns her and kisses the taut arc of her stomach. She grabs his hair and pulls his ear down, and her voice is a rush in his head.

Brazilian maids move in and out of their rooms after, transforming twisted sheets into fresh, flat ones, replacing towels, vacuuming and wiping traces of them clean until it is as if their trysts do not exist. This morning, when they came up from breakfast, a maid, a silhouette two doors up the hall, tried to ignore them as they kissed tightly in the hallway. His lover tugged at his shirt buttons, tugged at his belt as he tried to get the card in the slot, pulled his undershirt free as they went in the door.

She touches his fingers now, in the theater, tracing the topography of them; the man can almost believe that he too is a ghost, emerging, made into temporary flesh by her passion. It is amazing to him that he has pretended for so long that one doesn't need to feel what this woman kindles in him. He has an image of his wife, moving away from his body, his presence, in their spacious morning kitchen.

The harbor is very close, just off a boardwalk outside, and the man thinks he can feel it—high tide, the storm tossing the larger fishing boats at their berths, making them chafe and bite at the wharves. There is a wildness out there, in the night. There are millions of illicit lovers touching, millions of ghosts. The rain intensifies on the roof, and in the dim theater someone, a woman, exclaims at the sound. The curtain of glowing red velour remains closed. On either side of the stage are ceramic masks of triumph and tragedy, lit from below, shadows stabbing hugely onto the walls.

Now the lights go down. Outside the wind increases. A stay is rapping wildly against an aluminum mast, a broken slashing. The waves in the harbor are white. Seaport signs rattle and snap. The red curtain cleaves, and here in the hushed studio the actors emerge, shimmering; the orchestra plays something beautiful from another age. In this red, intense brightness, the man feels he is in the heart of some benevolent annihilation. There are things that he must work out, things he must think about; there must be some way for them to be together on some kind of steady basis.

But for now he watches with his lover, anticipating, with all of that story yet to come.

ACKNOWLEDGMENTS

I am greatly indebted to my mentor and friend, Andre Dubus, for his kindness and patience, and his profound influence on me. Andre helped edit a number of these stories, and after he left for the stars I continued to be guided by his voice. Some years later his son, Andre Dubus III, encouraged me as I started to collect these works. I have been blessed by the faith of father and son.

And I thank those friends who offered advice and support to me at other, critical times: David Brittan; Bill Cantwell; David Daniel; Nicole Delcourt; Susan Dodd; Carla Dragoni; Neenah Ellis; Patrice Gerrior; Carolyn Gregsak; Sylva Boyadjian-Haddad; Farid Haddad; Bill Henderson; Jack Herlihy; Lisabeth C. Kirk; Don Lee; Maggie Martin; Fatima and Jeremy McHugh; James Alan McPherson; Matt W. Miller; Michele Perkins; George Rosen; Sue Sawyer; Carolyn Seymour; Anita Shreve; Giselle Sterling; Rachael Stewart; Carol Thomas; Enid Thuermer, and Christopher Tilghman. My gratitude goes out to all of these generous people.

I thank my friends, fellow students, and teachers at the Iowa Writers' Workshop, and also the Thursday Nighters, who gathered with me to share stories, so many years ago, in Andre's home.

Finally, a big thank you to my family—for their constant faith, support, and strength.—JH

Made in the USA
Middletown, DE
13 November 2015